OUTLAWS NEVER DIE

THE DEVIL'S OUTLAWS
BOOK 5

BETHANY DAWN

To Kiki
Thank you for checking on me the last few months and always being ready to step into my chaotic mind to figure these characters out. Miles and Finn say they miss you, but don't tell anyone. Huntley is violent.

TRIGGER WARNINGS

This is a series about a 1%er motorcycle club, please expect them to act accordingly. Outlaws Never Die depicts extreme acts of violence, murder, recreational drug use, kidnapping, violence against the main female character by main male character, drugging of female main character, fertility issues and miscarriage for side character, surprise pregnancy, and explicit sex scenes. Please be conscious of your triggers, your mental health matters.

Bethany

PLAYLIST

Morning - Teyana Taylor, Kehlani
Love Lies - Khalid, Normani
Blastoff - Internet Money
Unholy - Sam Smith, Kim Petra
One of the Girls - The Weeknd, JENNIE, Lily Rose-Depp
Drugs & Money (New Mix) - Chase Atlantic
Goosebumps - Travis Scott
Lucid Dreams - Juice WRLD
Under The Influence - Chris Brown
Pictures on My Wall - Lithe

PLAYLIST AVAILABLE ON SPOTIFY @BETHANYDAWNN17

PROLOGUE

REYNA

"SO NOW YOU UNDERSTAND WHY," HE STATES, LICKING HIS LIPS.

And men say women are the emotionally unstable ones. I roll my eyes. This is a waste of my time. Men aren't complicated. They're fragile when their ego is threatened, so you stroke it, make them feel like the biggest and baddest man in the room, and viola, doors and wallets open.

"I don't care why," I finally say.

"So you'll do it?" He cocks his head, his brown eyes watching me.

"Yes," I answer plainly, pushing away from the table and standing.

"Send updates," he says dismissively.

Rolling my eyes, I turn on my heel to leave the house. "If I see fit."

He moves so silently that I don't realize he's stood and rounded the table, shoving me against the wall, my cheek slamming into it as his hand squeezes the back of my neck.

His hot breath fans over the side of my face. "All you are is a hired whore. You answer to me."

My arms are free, arrogant man, so I smash my elbow into his side, making him release my throat and step backward.

Spinning around, I grab him by the balls and squeeze, using the force to walk him back to the chair I vacated. "If you ever lay hands on me again, I will bring every resource I have down on you, and don't forget where I worked. I know a lot of important people who owe me favors."

He glares at me. "None that can tell you what I know," he grits through his teeth.

I squeeze harder, glaring at him with the same amount of hostility. I don't like him, and I won't pretend to. He finally yelps, and I let go triumphantly and walk peacefully out of the house.

Arrogant men will never understand that they don't run this world, women do, and we use them as our puppets.

He's just another means to an end. They all are.

1

LEO

MY HEART BEATS WILDLY IN MY CHEST AS I WATCH REYNA SAUNTER through the strip club. My palms grow slick against the armrests that I'm squeezing, my eyes glued to her swaying hips.

She looks a lot better than she did the day we found her on that island with Allie. Her hair is shiny and hanging down her back in loose waves, her makeup is perfect with a deep red lipstick that makes her plump lips even sexier. I feel kind of bad checking her out right now, since the last time I saw her she had makeup running down her face from crying and was practically naked and tied to a bed, but the moment I laid my eyes on her then, I was mesmerized. I've never seen a more beautiful woman, and I felt this intense urge to protect her. To shield her from whatever she had been through and to never let another man lay their hands on her.

It scared the ever loving fuck out of me.

I'm not possessive. I'm not protective.

I didn't care when Mase and I would pass Jessica back and forth before he met Allie and never touched another girl. I don't care when girls tell me we have to be discreet because they have a boyfriend and he can't find out about us. I didn't feel this way when I sat with Peyton at the hospital after the Kings had beaten her.

Don't get me wrong, I was upset about what happened to her, and I wanted the Kings to get what they were owed, but it was nothing compared to when I saw Reyna tied to that bed, mascara and eyeliner trailing down her cheeks and smudged lipstick, her eyes wide in fight.

The only woman I've ever felt anything similar to this... is Huntley. Or my mom, but that's a given.

Huntley, though... Huntley is a kindred soul. I see a lot of myself in her and a lot of her in me. We have a lot in common. Her mom left when she was young, my dad left. We both grew up in one-parent households where our parents loved us more than we could ever imagine. They sacrificed and made sure that we never felt the absence of our other parent. Or at least they tried, but I know Huntley still missed her mom.

Not me though. Fuck the man that left my mom.

My feelings for Huntley have never been romantic, though. Fuck, never that! She's my platonic soulmate, and I'll protect her if Finn ever can't.

Now Reyna... There's nothing platonic about the way I feel about her.

"Leo," Jack clears his throat, and I snap my head to the side to look at him.

His eyes are narrowed as he looks at me out of the side of his eyes.

My eyes slide in front of me. Reyna leans against the stage, her arms rest behind her as her legs extend out toward me. She cocks her head as she stares at me. Her ice blue eyes are eerie but captivating. She doesn't smile, just watches me. And I don't know... something creeps into the back of my head. Something feels wrong, but I don't know what.

"What?" I ask, looking back at Jack. Lost in my thoughts, I think I stared at Reyna the entire time.

"Reyna wants to audition," he states plainly. Everything he does lacks any emotion, but that's just who he is. To the point.

Oh god. It's hard to breathe when she's walking in tight jeans and a cropped tank top. Her dancing in pasties and panties will literally be the death of me.

"Why?" I blurt out, because I literally can't think of anything else to say.

Reyna's dark brows gather in the center, and her eyes narrow.

"Obviously for a job," she snaps, and Jack unsuccessfully covers a laugh by turning his head away from us. That's unlike him. Laughing in front of anyone other than me or Mase. Asshole.

"Do you have any experience dancing?" I ask, ignoring Jack as he watches Reyna and me with glee.

"You remember I worked in a brothel, right?" she pauses and sighs, like she's remembering the horrors of where we found her, which ended up being her former workplace. She wasn't completely upfront with us when we found her, but she came around and told Saint everything when she asked him to take her in. Maybe that's why I'm hesitant. She worked for our enemy. "I did a lot of pole dancing at the club. It was something to set me apart from the other girls," she says, pulling me from my thoughts once again.

I nod once, not really sure what else to say. I've never... thought so much regarding a woman. Either I like her or I don't. Either I go after her or I don't. Either we fuck or we don't.

Reyna's just not that simple, and I don't know what the fuck is going on with my head.

Jack gives me another odd glance out of the corner of his eyes. "Locker room is through those doors." He points to the back of the club. "And the DJ will play whatever song you want." Reyna pushes away from the stage and strides to the doors, and I let out a heavy breath, my eyes glued to her swaying hips again.

"What is going on with you?" Jack asks.

"I have no idea." I shake my head.

"I don't know if I trust her," Jack says quietly.

2

REYNA

Leo is predictable. I see it written all over his face. When you work so intimately with so many people for so long, you learn to read people. Body language, changes in tones, or speech. He's used to getting everything he wants and something about me has rocked him to his core, but I'm not sure what about me yet? Every time I walk into a room, he stops. Jack is a little harder. He's shut down, and the only one that can truly crack him open is Leo. They're always in a corner with their heads together, whispering or watching each other and communicating with just their eyes. It's clear they're close.

Now onto the clubhouse. I'm used to living in a dorm-like place, but the clubhouse differs greatly from La Lujuria. I lived there, even when the other girls didn't. They went home at the end of the night, but I stayed. I was always there. I had a bigger suite than the other girls. Mine had a living room, and the chef made my dinners every night before clients came in and breakfast every morning after they left.

The clubhouse does not have a chef, that's for damn sure. I thought I was going to catch something when I walked in, but

I'm coming around to its... charms. The guys are nice, loud sometimes, but they're reserved around me.

Allie hovers, which is annoying, but I know she does it because of how we met.

Huntley is pleasant. She doesn't talk too much and sometimes we just sit in silence and sip wine. I like her. And she helped me deep clean my room.

Reese judges me when she's not glued to her husband's side.

The locker room in the back of the strip club is basic, but clean. Flat, dark gray walls with a dark wood floor. It's lighter and cleaner feeling than the main room of the club, with its black walls and dark tiled floor. Leo and Jack were sitting in the chairs around the pole in the middle of the room.

I wonder if they'll dim the lights for my audition or if they'll keep the bright overhead lights on. It's not very flattering, but it won't really matter. I'll pass this regardless of the lights.

In the open, I pull my shirt over my head and stuff it into the small duffle bag I carried in here, then I pull off my jeans and thong and shove them in along with my top, shuffling around in the bag for a pair of black, high-waisted boy shorts. The plain outfit isn't anything special, but I didn't want to go overboard just for this, plus I don't know what their dress code is. The black bralette that barely contains my breasts and the boy shorts that show a lot of ass are a safe option.

Digging to the bottom of the bag, I grab my heels and look over them, memories rushing through my head. These were the shoes I wore when I started at La Lujuria. They were the first pair of designer heels I bought with my first paycheck, but I quickly replaced them. I don't think my other heels would be suitable for the pole, so I chose these old, black Louboutin Bianca pumps. They are far from normal stripper heels, but they have the height of the platform, so they'll do for now. I'll head to a store after this for real heels.

Dropping the shoes to the floor, I slip my feet into them and walk out of the locker room.

A slight chill rushes over me as I step into the main room, but I ignore it as I walk to the DJ booth to tell the MC my song choice.

He nods as I give him the name and he waits until I've taken my place at the base of the stage. Leaning against the stage like before, I rest my ass against the cold ledge and grip the lip with my hands. Looking between Leo and Jack, I decide that I'll dance for Leo. I nod to the DJ and the sultry beats of my song thump through the club.

Pushing off of the stage, my hips pop to the beat of "Morning" by Teyana Taylor and Kehlani as I slowly walk toward Leo, circling around him once, lightly dragging my hand over his shoulder, only my middle finger actually making contact with his soft tee shirt. At his side, I drop to a quick squat, my eyes on him the entire time.

Leo's head turns to the side, his eyes following me. His hands rest on the arms of the chair in fists as he runs his tongue over his top lip.

With my other hand, I reach for his chest and run my hand down his stomach while I pop my ass and move my hips to the beat. His stomach muscles jump as my hand gently glides down his body and I smile internally at his reaction to my touch. This is going to be so easy.

Standing, I move in front of him, spinning once along the way. Bending forward, I sway my hips and push his legs further apart. I place my hands on his shoulder and step onto the chair in between his legs.

His eyes widen and his hands grip onto my ankles, like he thinks I'll fall. I want to roll my eyes. I don't need his help. Instead, I lower my lids, creating a sort of siren gaze and slightly part my lips as I look down at him.

The chill of the room has been replaced with the warmth of adrenaline. Dancing is what I always enjoyed at La Lujuria. It was my escape, my time to myself. Even though it looked like a time for others, like I was doing these moves to please others, I was doing it for me. Moving my body felt good. I did the moves that made me feel sexy, and I got off on the reactions of others. The envy from the other girls, the lust and admiration from the clients. It was pure self satisfaction disguised as service.

I was the best, and I fucking knew it. That wouldn't change here.

Moving my hips in circles, I slowly drop to a squat again, tossing my head around and pushing my chest into Leo's face. The long wisps of my back hair sweep around Leo and I and they tickle along my bare shoulders and back.

Stepping down, I turn away from Leo and slide onto my butt, one leg bent and the other extended in front of me. I fall onto my back and lift my legs above my head and backward onto Leo.

His big hands squeeze the back of my thighs as I grab the legs of the chair and lift myself onto Leo. I continue the motion until I'm upright and sitting on Leo's lap.

I lean against him, the beat of his chest burning through his shirt, and roll my body against his, turning my head and running my nose along his tanned neck. Goosebumps erupt along his skin, and I know that this is going better than I could have even imagined. To further push this, I replace my nose with my tongue and lick a small train the rest of the way to his jaw.

Out of the corner of my vision, I see his hands move from the armrest, so I push off his body before he can grab me.

With the beat, I walk to the stage and take the stairs up and walk around the back of the pole. I place my back against it and slide down to my butt. Tossing my hair around, I move onto my knees and crawl around to the front of the pole, sliding onto my stomach and moving my arms above my head. Leo leans forward, his eyes narrowing on me as I bite my lip and watch him. His eyes travel down my body and I can physically feel them like they're his hands instead.

Pushing back onto my butt, I move to my knees again and grab the pole, using it to stand and walk around it.

Gripping onto the pole, I toss my body around it, my legs leaving the floor and snapping into a wide straddle, landing to the side. I body roll against the pole a few times before I climb the pole, spinning and working my body to the beat. I use my hair as an extension of my dancing and flip my hair around as I spin on the pole.

Once at the top, I invert and open my legs, bracketing the pole, holding that for a beat before bending my knees and moving my legs like a wave. My legs wrap around the pole again and I twist, tucking the pole between my legs and resting against my ass to transition into the Archer pose, the pole running along my back, with one ankle wrapped around it and the other leg tucked into my stomach, upside down again.

Sliding my legs up the pole, I let go with my hands and hold the Ankle Hang, with my hands outstretched to the side and slowly let myself slide down the pole until my hands can touch the floor.

Holding my weight, I let go of the pole with my legs and push off of it, sliding into a split in front of the pole to end my dance.

My chest heaves as I turn out of my split and face the front where Leo and Jack are sitting. The two women who were at the bar when I walked in have come to the stage and are standing behind Jack and Leo.

Jack's brows are raised slightly while Leo's chest rises just as quickly as mine, and his face looks slightly pale.

"Fucking wow," one women laughs, her mouth hanging open. "She's hired, right?"

Jack smirks, his head turning toward Leo. "I don't know, Leo, what do you think?"

Leo clears his throat roughly and blinks, his eyes screwing shut. "Yeah, Reyna's hired." He pushes out of his chair and walks to the bar.

I push off of the floor of the stage and walk to the stairs. "You start tomorrow at ten," Jack says loudly enough for me to hear. Raising my hand in acknowledgement, I walk back to the locker room to change.

3

REYNA

I HEFT THE STRAP OF MY SMALL DUFFLE HIGHER ON MY SHOULDER as I step out of the club, looking around the parking lot. I didn't expect Archer to stick around and wait for me, but he could have at least said he wouldn't wait. We're not friends, I would say, but he is helpful when I need something. My own car would be really nice right about now, but I don't have a license. I never got it. I rarely left the island, and when I did, the club had a driver for me.

I take my phone out of my bag and pull up Huntley's number, pressing dial.

"What's up?" she answers.

"Do you want to go shopping with me? I could kind of use a ride." A sudden breeze whispers by, tossing my hair to the side and causing goosebumps to rise on my arms. Fall is coming soon, and I'm not going to be able to wear my thin strapped crop tops by themselves for too much longer.

"Sure. Are you at the clubhouse? Finn! I'm going to hang out with Reyna for a while!" Huntley calls on the other end.

"No. I'm at the Second Circle. The strip club," I answer, examining my nails. I need to get these redone as well. They're a little grown out. I haven't had a lot of time to do maintenance while I was lying low with an FBI agent and then moving into a grown-up version of a frat house. Barf.

Huntley pauses. "Why are you at the strip club?"

"I got a job."

She chuckles and I hear a car door shut. "Okay. I'm on my way!"

I say goodbye to Huntley and hang up. The strip club is on the outskirts of town, so there isn't anything else out here. I don't really want to go back inside and wait for her, so I lean against the rough brick wall to wait.

"Where are we going?" Huntley asks as I open the door to her Jaguar and get in.

"Isn't there a stripper supply store in Merrill Hill?" I close the door and pull the seatbelt down over me.

She backs out and nods. "Yeah, Ecstasy," she answers. We get a few yards from the club and she speaks up again. "Why'd you go to the club for a job?"

I stare out the window at the passing trees and buildings, but still answer. "I used to dance at my old club. I'm good, so I figured I'd keep doing it."

"Being in an environment like that won't trigger anything from the night your club was attacked?" she asks cautiously, quietly.

I shake my head. "I don't think so. I got out before anything happened and was able to take some of my stuff. Dancing was always an escape for me; I don't want to give that up."

She nods, her eyes on the road ahead of us. "Well, if you want to practice, there's a pole studio in town that I go to a few times a week."

And that's it. Neither of us needs to say anything else. I nod and the conversation ends. That's why I enjoy being with Huntley. She doesn't need to fill every moment with pointless conversation. We can just exist together.

"Do you know what the dress code is?" I ask, pushing open the door to the cute boutique. "I forgot to ask."

She side-eyes me, her blue gaze falling down, then back up my body while I grab a mesh shopping bag at the door. "It's a strip club. Isn't naked the dress code?"

Rolling my eyes, I flick through a rack of costumes. "No, some clubs are fully nude, others are topless. Some require you to wear cocktail dresses while not on stage." I grab a few costumes, since I saw a theme night poster in the locker room.

"Oh. Uhh. It's a topless club, and the girls usually walk around in their dancing outfits when not on stage. I think. I haven't been there a lot," she answers, flipping through the costumes and pausing on a little angel one.

"I'll order my lingerie online then, but I need shoes and some costumes." I turn around and see the giant shoe display at the back of the shop.

While I'm scanning the display shoes, the sales attendant walks over to us. "I'll take the thigh high leather boots without the laces in black, the open toe heels in black, clear, and red," I pause, continuing to scan the wall. "And the black heels with the blacklight, orange glitter pumpkin face, since Halloween is soon." I stare at her as she watches me, not moving. "Thanks." I tack on so she'll get going.

Huntley laughs from beside me. "How festive."

"Fuck off," I chuckle as well. And the feeling of friendship and lightness feels foreign to me. I don't know if I've ever had a true friend. I try to think back. I haven't. All of my 'friends' have been the men that I worked for. I don't consider the girls I worked with friends. We worked together and competed against one another. I was in charge of them. We weren't friends.

Taking my basket to the counter, I wait for the sales attendant to ring up my items. Huntley buys the angel costume and helps me carry the shoe boxes out to her car.

"You know," Huntley starts as we're driving down the road. "I teach self-defense classes in my studio. You should come by sometime. It wouldn't hurt to have some knowledge of defending yourself if you're going to be working at the club." I turn and give her an assessing glare and she continues. "Or just come by to let out some steam on my kickboxing bags."

"I'll think about it," I say as she pulls up to the clubhouse gate and types in the code for the gates.

4

LEO

Pop! Pop! Pop! I FIRE OFF ROUNDS, HITTING THE TARGET EVERY time.

"Your groupings are getting better," Finn grunts from behind me.

Nodding, I step aside, letting Finn step up to the plate to hit his own target. "Do you miss me at the shop?" I ask, bending down to grab my bottle of water from the deep green grass. The trees lining Finn's backyard, doubling as a fence, stand tall as the wind ruffles their leaves. It's almost October and the leaves should turn soon. I know it's such a womanly thing to say, but I fucking love fall. The vibrant orange and yellow leaves pop against the deep green evergreens. The comfortable breeze with the views on a bike? There's nothing better. Then when the rain comes, we have to put our bikes away for the year. That sucks.

"Yes." He pulls the trigger four times in a quick succession, hitting the bullseye each time. "I very much miss telling you to work on something and then finding you in the office gossiping with my Old Lady."

"I bet she misses me," I mock, stepping up as he steps back again.

"Motherfucker!" he snaps, and I sidestep away from his hand that's barreling toward me with a laugh.

"I'm joking." I take my place, still laughing at his glowering face. He knows it's not like that between me and Huntley. It's never not funny to give him shit though. Five more shots, and I let Finn take my place. "But I do know Jack is missing working in the garage."

Finn fires his rounds and then steps forward to replace the paper target, and I follow.

"Oh, he doesn't like the strip club?" he asks, his long legs eating up the grass.

I scoff. "You know naked women make him uncomfortable. I'm pretty sure he's a virgin."

Finn barks out a laugh, ripping the target from the board and replacing it with a clean one. "Easy pussy surrounds the two of you every day. There's no way he's still a virgin."

"He's not." I replace my target and turn around to follow Finn back to the shooting point. "People just make him uncomfortable and at the shop he didn't have to deal with them."

Finn nods. "I do miss you guys at the shop. Well, I miss Jack. He was a good worker." He purses his lips, no doubt holding in a smile.

"Fuck you," I laugh, shaking my head. "We've been doing auditions for new dancers, but after this, I think he'll just come in a few nights to do the books and I'll take care of everything else."

"Saint definitely knew where to put you. If anything will get you to work, it's pussy." Finn laughs at his own joke and we finish out our magazines, taking turns.

"Where's Noctem?" I ask, looking around for the medium-sized ball of fluff. I thought at some point she would join us out here like she usually does.

Finn picks up his spent casings next to me and drops them into a plastic bag. "Inside begging for food. She barely leaves Huntley's side, but especially not when she's cooking." Chuckling, I drop my casings in the bag along with Finn's. These will go to the warehouse to make new bullets that we'll then sell. "Do you wanna stay for dinner?" he asks, sealing the bag and standing.

"Sure." I shrug. Huntleys an excellent cook and it beats what I was going to do, which was go home and order a pizza while I tore out my bathroom.

The cabin is pretty dated, and at first it didn't bother me, but the more time I spent there, I decided I wanted to modernize the place a little. Mostly just the bathrooms and kitchen, maybe fix the dock too. It's a little rickety.

Finn slides the glass door open, and we step inside. Noctem barks, but only once. "It's okay, Noxy, it's just Daddy," Huntley soothes from the stove.

Noctem's paws tap against the wood floors as she trots to us, getting a head scratch from Finn and sniffing me.

"Hey sweet girl, did you miss Uncle Leo?" I bend down to kiss her snout and stroke her soft head. She's grown so much since Finn bought her. From a little chunky potato into a fierce guard dog for Huntley. And she goes everywhere with her. To the shop, the clubhouse, follows her around the house. I think the only place she doesn't go is the grocery store, and that's probably because she'd bite the first person who accidentally bumped into Huntley.

"Are you staying for dinner, Leo?" Huntley asks, turning her head and accepting a kiss from Finn.

"Yeah, that okay?" I kick my shoes off at the back door and walk to the counter, placing my gun case down.

"Of course. I'm just fluffing the rice and then we can eat," Huntley says, focused on her 'fluffing.'

"Smells delicious, Angel. We'll go wash up." Finn gives Huntley another kiss to her temple as a goodbye.

I don't miss the times before Cale, Finn, Saint, and Mason were shacked up with their women. Okay, that's kind of a lie. I do miss Mason a bit, but honestly, once he got Allie in his sight, he wasn't any fun anymore.

I think Reese and Huntley helped Cale and Finn a lot, bringing out their best qualities and mellowing them out. Allie has helped Saint a lot too, but there was a time when I thought he was going to murder her. Now they're good, and I've never seen Mason happier than when he's with Allie. God, he's going to be insufferable when they get back from their honeymoon. Only a few more days.

"So you hired Reyna?" Huntley asks as we're seated around the dining table. I nod, swallowing a huge bite of the chicken taco soup. Fuck, this is good. "You'll make sure no one crosses a line with her, right?"

I squeeze the fork harder at the thought of someone touching her. I know she's going to be touching guys, dancing on them, but we have a strict no touching rule—unless the dancer says otherwise. "Of course." I grunt. I should feel this passionately about protecting all of my dancers—and I *do* feel protective over their safety and comfortability—but it's different with Reyna. God, I'm going to have to watch her grind on guys' laps and shove her... really nice tits in their faces. Am I ready for that? Maybe I should have thought about that before I hired her, but I wasn't thinking that far ahead, and everyone else was saying how great she was. And she was. How could I say no after a dance like that? She's the type of dancer that you beg to work in your club, the type that you do everything you can to get her.

"Okay." She nods, turning to her dinner.

"You two have become good friends," I state. I've noticed

them talking at club dinners, but now Reynas telling her about her job? Jack or I didn't tell her.

"Yeah." Huntley nods, a small smile pulling at her bare lips. "I like her, and we seem to be a lot alike. She called me after her audition and we went shopping. It was fun."

Finn smirks across the table from her, his giant bowl already half gone. "That's where you got that outfit?"

Huntley giggles, fucking giggles. "Mhmm," she hums, her smile growing wider as she looks down at her bowl. Only Finn could make her act like this. She's reserved and serious around everyone else, but Finn comes in and opens her up. Like a blooming flower opening for the morning sun.

We eat the rest of our dinner, making small conversation about the projects Finn's doing at the shop, Noctem, and what Jack and I plan to do with the club since we've taken it over. Tobi used to run it, and it was an okay place, but Jack and I have a vision for it.

We want to give it more of a vibe. I don't know. Right now it's just... vibeless. God, that sounds stupid, but it's true. The music sucks, the lighting is trash, the furniture is gaudy. It doesn't feel like thought went into the interior at all.

And we're wanting to bring in an additional source of revenue for the club. Alcohol in strip clubs is banned in the state of Washington. That shit doesn't make sense to Jack or I. We could increase the money that is spent on the girls, increasing their pay, and increase the revenue for the strip club with the sale of alcohol, which of course increases the money that the overall club makes since the club owns Second.

Brilliant plan, we just have to figure out how to do it and run it by Saint and the rest of the club.

"That's a great idea! It felt weird to go into a strip club and order a soda," Huntley says, glancing at Finn.

He shrugs, "Didn't bother me none, but it would be good for the club."

I snort, rolling my eyes. "Yeah, because the bar was always stocked for club members, but regular customers would appreciate it."

"Yeah." Finn nods. "You should definitely figure out the logistics and bring it up at the next church."

I help Finn clean off the table after dinner, and leave their house excited for the future of Second, while also nervous about how next weekend would go. Our official reopening.

5

REYNA

My room is so basic, as in all that's in here are the basics. A bed and a dresser. There was a desk, but I'm positive whoever was in this room before me fucked girls on it. The mattress too obviously—but I replaced that. Huntley told me that was a good idea. I did what I could. Nice bedding, soft lighting, and candles, but there's only so much I could do. There's no quick fix for cheap, low pile carpet and dingy white walls.

I hate it here, but this is the best place for me, at least for now.

I don't have a lot of clothes since I only made it out of La Lujuria with a few pieces, but I've bought and ordered a few things since being here.

But since I still don't have much, my dresser is mostly empty. So I place the costumes I bought for the club into the top drawer from my laundry basket. Tiny tops and bottoms, some with accessories. The lingerie and practice wear I ordered should be here soon. I wanted decent quality materials, and the stuff at the shop was not that. It was probably better for sweating and working, but I was used to luxury lingerie. I didn't want to give that

25

up. Though what I bought for my dances wasn't luxury, it was a little better than what the shop had.

Resentment for my situation flares inside of me. My life was fine before. My job was fine. People respected me; now I'm here.

The sooner I get this over with, the better.

But I don't know what I'll do after I leave this place behind. Where I'll go. Maybe New York. Or Dubai.

Piling my long hair onto my head in a bun, I crawl onto my bed and pick up my laptop to search songs for some sets. Jack said that Second was having a grand reopening, so I want to have some routines in mind. Maybe I'll take Huntley up on her offer to hit up the pole studio for some practice before the opening in a week.

The clubhouse is quiet. I mean, only Jack and I live here, and most of the guys don't really come around unless something is going on. They all have jobs or a home. Even Sunday dinners are at Saint, Allie, and Mason's house.

Two husbands, Jesus Christ, who the fuck would want that?

The amount of times I had a client come in and complain about their significant other was enough to tell me I wasn't missing anything by never being in a relationship.

Although there was a man that I thought I had liked at one point. He was a security guard at La Lujuria. I wasn't quite eighteen, so I was doing the client intake forms, working with the girls, administration things. We used to meet in the kitchen and eat together, hide in a quiet corner away from everyone else, and talk about things. He told me what Seattle was like and the world outside of Martin Island. He was sweet, and he listened to me, looked out for me, and brought me things from the city.

I knew I was going to move into the entertaining side of La Lujuria when I turned eighteen—my choice—and the last thing I wanted to do was lose my virginity to a gross old man who smelled like cigars.

I thought maybe we could build something together. Maybe I'd leave the island to be with him.

It turned out there was a bet going on of who could break down my walls first. A pretty hefty payout.

La Reina de la lujuria.

The queen of lust.

The queen of La Lujuria.

That's what I was: a prize.

When I became the top earner. When I earned my place at the top, I had him fired. I couldn't stand to see his deceitful face every day.

And since then, I never needed anyone else.

So I don't mind the quiet here. I don't mind staying in this one room for the majority of my day. Jack and I keep to ourselves. We eat separately. He comes and goes without my knowledge. He doesn't bother me. I like it.

But the club dinners aren't horrible, and I enjoy spending time with Huntley. And Leo is fun to watch. The way he squirms when I enter the room; I enjoy it.

I've settled on a few songs, and I listen to them repeatedly, picturing routines in my mind. I'll call Huntley and ask to use the studio tomorrow so I can see if what I created in my mind will actually work together.

6

———

LEO

Why the fuck did I decide to buy a cabin in the middle of the fucking woods?

I had it all set up for myself. A free place to live that horny women just showed up to in groups. Though now that they've seen most of the brothers settling down with Old Ladies, a lot of them don't come around anymore.

We weren't like typical clubs, though. The cut sluts didn't live at the club or even come around every day. Most only come around when club events are going on, mostly parties. They are girls who just want to fuck and party with Outlaws, but they have lives outside of the club. Then there was Peyton, but she isn't a cut slut, she's family.

But anyway, now I have to do my laundry and cook for myself—something I was could usually get one of the girls to do for me. I decided to renovate arguably the hardest parts of a house, and I'm stuck doing yard work. Like picking up branches. Fuck raking leaves though, it's the fucking forrest, there's gonna be leaves and pinecones on the ground. I'd leave the branches too if I'm being honest, but I almost tripped over one the other night, so those fuckers have got to go; plus I can use them for fire kindling when it cools down.

In truth, I bought this place for Jack and I. When you prospect for the club, you live in the clubhouse, but once we patched in, I thought maybe we could move out and live together somewhere. But he didn't want to.

I was a little hurt by it, but I wasn't going to tell him that.

So it's just me out here, but it's okay.

I toss another branch into one of my piles I've made around the yard, and the rumble of a bike makes me turn around.

The bastard himself rolls down my dirt drive, his permanent disinterested face in perfect view.

He takes his helmet off and hangs it on his handlebar, running his hand through his short, bright blonde hair, making it stick up in spikes as he walks toward me.

"I never thought I'd see Leo Garcia doing yard work," he jokes, though if you didn't know him, you wouldn't think he was joking since he doesn't say it with a hint of amusement.

I twist my face mockingly. "Yeah, yeah, just fucking help me." I toss a stick at him.

He catches it and drops it onto the pile he's standing next to and helps me. "I think I know how to get liquor into the club, and it's completely legal."

"No shit?" I straighten and focus on him, crossing my sweaty arms. It's a great day. The sun is shining, but it's not hot, just comfortable with a light breeze—doesn't mean I didn't work up a sweat though. I *have* been cleaning up my yard for over an hour.

"We expand the club and place a liquor store next to it. There'll be a door to connect the two buildings, but they'll have to be two separate businesses." His mouth slides into his version of a smile—which is barely one at all—and he waits for me.

"But wouldn't it be obvious that we're serving alcohol in the club?" I ask, not following his plan at all. Sounds terrible to me.

He shakes his head and walks toward me. "We're not serving alcohol. The customers are buying it in a fully legal liquor store and bringing it into the club. The law says we can't serve or sell alcohol, not that we can't allow it into the building." His smile grows into a smirk as my eyes go wide with realization. That's fucking genius! Only one problem...

"An expansion won't be done by the time of our grand opening next week, and a business license and liquor license on top of that," I counter.

He sighs and turns away to grab a branch. "Yeah, we'd have to operate illegally until the store is finished and legal. But the club is open at night, and the construction would take place during the day, so we wouldn't have to shut down until it was finished."

Nodding, I add another few branches to the pile while I think about Jack's plan. "I think this could work, and it's not like we're not used to running illegal shit. I think we should bring this up in church when Saint and Mason get back tomorrow."

"That's what I was hoping you'd say, brother." Jack grins—for him—and continues to help me pick up the branches until the yard is mostly clean of them.

We combine the piles into bigger ones and set them near the house so I can use them come winter. Then we head inside and Jack grills some steaks for us on my grill on the deck.

This was what I imagined when I bought this house. My brother and I are just living our lives as we wanted. No one to answer to, and just having a chill fucking time together.

I would be lying if I said I didn't want to ask him about Reyna, though, during the quietness of our dinner together, but I didn't. Because I don't need to know what she's up to. She's just a girl the club took in because we owed her, nothing more.

7

LEO

"Welcome back, brother." Finn claps a smiling Saint on the back and he nods.

"I missed you, brother." I hug Mase, whose smile almost splits his face. It's so wide. Both Saint and Mason look a lot lighter and happier than they did a month ago. I never thought I'd see two brothers married to one girl, but it works for them, so I'm stoked for the couple. Or throuple? I don't fucking know.

Who would have thought one girl could bring these two opposite men together and complete them?

It's also pretty fucking weird to see a wedding ring on Mase's finger. He's a few years older than me, but we came into the club at the same time. We did everything together, and now he's married and living in a big house overlooking the water. He's got everything all set up for himself.

"Where's Cale?" Saint asks as Jack closes the chapel doors.

"Doctor's appointment with the Princess ran a little late. He's on his way," Finn answers, walking to his seat.

We gather around the chapel table, and to see empty seats is the most gut wrenching feeling.

Everyday we are reminded of the absence of Ronan, Tobi,

Nate, and even Wyatt, but it becomes more real when we see the physical evidence that they are no longer here. I look around at my remaining brothers. Those deaths could have been any of us. It could have been me. It could have been Jack or Mase.

I don't blame Wyatt for getting the fuck out of here. He never would have healed if he had stayed. Sometimes I wish I would have stayed with him in California—I even talked to Jack about it—but he wouldn't budge, and I couldn't leave him. We came into this club together and we'll go out together.

Speaking of gut wrenching feelings, the ghosts seem to have faded from Saint's eyes, and I know that has to do with his new Old Lady and finally putting Ronan's murderer in the ground.

"So what's happened over the last two weeks? I didn't get any calls while we were gone, so no one was arrested." Saint leans back in his chair at the head of the table, twisting his wedding ring around his finger.

"We hired new management for Whiskey Springs, and we got Marlene and the kids all packed up for their move to Tennessee," Finn says.

Saint nods. "Good. Nate would appreciate Whiskey Springs staying in the club, and I know Tobi would appreciate getting his wife and kids back near her parents." He purses his lips, looking down at the table. "I should have been here to help with that."

Finn shakes his head. "No, brother. You were where they would have wanted you to be. The club took care of everything; It's okay."

The door opens and Cale walks in, his mood shifting the entire room in an instant.

"Hey, everything okay, Cale?" Finn asks, his deep blue eyes following the surly Sergeant at Arms.

Callum deftly lands in his chair between Saint and Mason. "No." He shakes his head. Everyone sits in bated breath, waiting to see if he'll elaborate. Finally, he does. He sighs. "Reese missed her period this month, so we went in to see, and it was negative. She went off birth control after we moved in together, and we weren't exactly trying, but we weren't trying not to either. The doctor ran some tests, but he said the chances of Reese getting pregnant probably weren't very great. He said he'd know for sure when he got the tests back." His eyes mist over as he glares at the table. "She already miscarried once, so she's pretty torn up right now."

"Fuck, Callum, why didn't you tell us?" Finn asks.

"It was still early when we found out. She didn't want to tell anyone yet, and then..." he trails off, squeezing his eyes shut and turning his head to the side.

Saint leans forward and clasps his hand on Cale's shoulder. "Go home, brother. We can text you."

"Can you drive?" I ask. I don't know what else to say. I feel fucking sick for Cale and Reese, but I've never even had a serious girlfriend, let alone a family I'm trying to build.

"Yeah." He nods, his eyes still closed as he takes a deep breath. "I'm just trying to be strong right now, so she knows she doesn't have to be."

"You don't have to be strong with us," Finn says, his voice a little gravelly.

Cale opens his eyes, the mist gone and his resolve back. "I know, but not right now." He stands from the table. "Call me if there's anything I need to know. I'll be home for a few days with Red."

We all say our goodbyes and watch him leave, my heart shattering once again for one of my brothers. Fuck, when are things going to turn around for us?

We sit in silence for a moment. When one of us hurts, we all hurt.

"Mase," Saint says.

"Yep, already texting Allie, but I'm sure Reese already told her," Mason answers, looking down at his phone in his lap.

"Leave them alone tonight, but you two should go over tomorrow night, and Finn and I can take Cale to Big Dawgs for a drink," Saint says to Mason, but glances at Finn at the end.

"I'll ask Dad to shut down Big Dawgs for us," Finn confirms, nodding.

"Jack, Leo, you can come too," Saint adds.

I nod, looking at Jack—who nods once as well. "Of course we'll be there," I answer for the both of us.

"Okay," Saint sighs. "Anything else? Any progress with Second?"

"Yeah," I clear my throat. "We've finished auditions, hired three new dancers, and we're getting the place redone for the reopening this weekend." I pause, watching Saint nod his approval. "We also thought of a way to bring in a new revenue stream..." I explain the plan Jack came up with, and everyone thought it was great.

We know the implications of running it illegally for the first month or so, but it's not worse than running illegal ammo. Saint said we could go forward with the liquor store, but not until after the grand reopening. We at least want to have the first weekend without the construction tape and plastic put up.

church is adjourned, and we all stand and leave the chapel. Finn and Saint leave to head back to work, but Jack, Mase, and I take a seat at the bar to catch up.

"How's the married life?" I ask, unscrewing the cap on a bottle of orange juice.

"Good." Mason's warm smile seems to make his entire body vibrate with happiness. "Busy, but good. There isn't ever a dull moment when there's three people in the marriage."

"Yeah, I bet Allie feels really *full* of love," I smirk and Jack chokes on his water beside me, but Mason takes my raunchy jokes in stride like he always has and chuckles.

"Any other brother would knock your ass out for talking about their Old Lady like that," he shakes his head and smiles.

"Yeah, but you're a pussy," I snap, barking a laugh as I rush off of my stool, dodging his fist.

I push through the door into the kitchen and come to an abrupt halt. Reyna looks over her bare shoulder at me from the stove. Her black hair hangs loose down her back, a white bralette peeking through the strands and barely covering her full back piece, the black lines of the tattoo swirling over her smooth skin. The tight black spandex shorts she wears end just under her plump ass and her long soft legs stand strong beneath her.

I feel the familiar feeling of my throat closing and my heart rate jacking up. That's become normal when I'm in her presence.

She turns around without a word and goes back to her cooking; her tattooed arm stirring eggs in a skillet.

I try to clear my throat as quietly as possible as I walk over to the industrial fridge.

The spatula clanks against the porcelain plate before I feel her tits press against my back and her arm reaches around my body. My spine snaps straight, and all the air leaves my lungs, her lustful cherry scent filling them instead.

"For someone so confident you seem to lose all of your bravado anytime you see me," she purrs, and I close my eyes. My dick hardens in my jeans and I'm torn because fuck her for noticing what's happening to me, but also I really want to fuck her.

I open my eyes to the sound of her grabbing something in the fridge and see her manicured hand retreat with the ketchup, and then she pulls away from me as quietly as she came.

I turn around and watch her sway her perfect ass to her plate. She smirks as she turns around with it in her hand and walks toward the door.

"Bye, pet," she coos, pushing the door open and leaving me with just my raging thoughts and hard on.

Yanking open the freezer, I step as close as possible, hoping the cold will calm me.

Fuck her. Literally and figuratively.

8

LEO

I don't think I've ever seen the parking lot of Big Dawgs empty during normal business hours. The food is fucking spectacular and randy has a habit of making friends with anyone who steps through his doors. It's just the perfect place. Great atmosphere, great service, great food, and cold drinks.

Today, though, there are only four bikes parked out front, and the neon open sign is off.

"Closed for dinner." Is written on a sheet of printer paper and taped to the window of one of the front doors, and I swing it open. The smell of delicious fried food smacks me in the face as I step into the bar.

Two square tables have been pushed together in the middle of the dining area, and my brothers sit around them with Randy. Bottles of beer are passed around and everyone mingles, not even paying attention to me walking in.

"Fucking finally!" Finn shouts. "We were wasting away waiting for you!" he says as I sit down beside Jack.

"I'm so sure." I smirk at my VP across the table from me.

"Beer?" Randy asks, pushing to stand from the chair at the end of the table.

"Yeah." I nod. "Thank you."

Finn shoots out of his seat. "I got it, Dad." He pats Randy on the shoulder as he passes him. "Be ready to order by the time I get back!" he calls as he walks toward the bar.

Finn heads to the grill to help Randy make our food. We all ordered a meal plus an appetizer each, and when one of us runs out of beer or switches to soda or water, we get our own refills. We'll keep track of what we drink and make sure Randy is paid appropriately. Even though he'd shut the restaurant down and feed us for free without complaint, we would never do that to him.

Cale is quiet, and he chews on his lip while we wait for our food.

"Do you wanna talk about it?" Saint asks.

"Not really," Cale says sadly. "I just want to think about something else. Getting out and coming here where we've had so many good memories is helping."

Saint nods. "Mason said they were going to take Reese to the pier in Seattle and hit all the shops with desserts."

Cale lets out a soft chuckle. "She'll love that." His lips slide into a small smile under the whisper of a mustache. I've never seen him grow his facial hair out this much before.

"Mase and Allie thought so too." Saint watches him, his light blue eyes trained on him.

"Tell me about your honeymoon." Callum looks at me. "Or your bathroom reno. Just something light, please."

So we do. Saint tells us about the things the three newlyweds got up to. After their commitment ceremony in Singapore, they explored the city and traveled around, eventually ending up on the private Joyo Island. My renovation has been a lot less relaxing.

"Huntley said she hasn't seen any of your half naked dancing videos recently?" Finn says as he and Randy return with all the food.

"Yeah," I answer after swallowing the bite of my french dip. "I deleted the app after shit started getting real. It didn't feel like the time to take off my shirt and dance to some song on the internet." Saint chews on the inside of his lip and I know he's feeling guilty about the war we started. But none of us blames him for anything. There may have been a lot of collateral damage along the way, but we put Ronan's murderer in the ground, at least we got that.

Finn clears his throat. "So anyway, Noctem made a friend at the dog park this week," he changes the subject and we all listen while enjoying our food.

9

———

REYNA

"THANKS, ARCHER CANCELED ON ME AT THE LAST MINUTE TO PLAY pretend gangster," I say, sliding into Huntley's Jaguar.

"Fuck, Nox." She glares ahead, her hands tightening on the wheel.

"Who?" I ask, turning to grab the seat belt and fasten it over me.

She shakes her head, shifting gears and reversing out of the spot in the clubhouse parking lot. "Aren't you nervous about being friends with an undercover FBI agent? What if he's just gaining information on you?"

I shrug, glancing out the window at the passcode box as we pass through the compound gate. "I'm not friends with him because I enjoy his company. It's kind of a necessity right now. I don't have anyone else to lean on right now. Besides, I'm not escorting anymore, so there isn't anything of value he can get from me."

She stomps on the accelerator, our bodies jolting back into the seats. "Sorry," she chuckles. "Finn did something to the engine, and I wanted to check it out." She slows down to a normal speed and continues. "The club will take care of you. You don't need to rely on lying feds anymore."

"Okay." Like I said, I'm not friends with Archer because I actually like him. I just need a ride sometimes. I should just start using taxis; I don't like relying on others.

"So why do you have to go in tonight? Do you have to practice with the other dancers?" Huntley asks.

"No, it's a club meeting. I guess we're going to go over opening night." I watch the trees as we drive. On Martin Island there weren't a lot of trees. The island was mostly made up of helicopter landing pads, two boat docks, and the club; there wasn't room for much else. I always admired the trees from a distance, but to see them now, up close and in detail, is beautiful. There weren't this many trees in Seattle, but out here in Merrill Hill where life is slower and buildings are shorter, the trees tower over them: they look like they could reach the clouds.

It's beautiful here. Too bad I won't be staying.

I wave thanks to Huntley as I open the car door and step out, but I turn around as the engine turns off and a car door opens. She's getting out.

"I really want to see what Jack and Leo have done to the place." She steps out, clicking her key fob and striding toward the door.

I adjust my black, high-waisted jeans and follow Huntley into Second.

The overhead lights are on and I almost don't recognize the club. There are still the three stages, the main one in the middle and the other two are small and off to the side. They have replaced the tile flooring with a solid black floor that my heeled boots click against as I walk. Light strips line basically everywhere. A detailed criss cross design on the ceiling, around the stages and steps up to them, and under the bar. They painted the walls with black glitter, and replaced the chairs with shorter round ones. These are sleeker than the old ones.

The bar has also undergone an upgrade—though I'm not really sure of its purpose— with a long mirror outlined with the same lights stretching the length of the wall. Stools at the bar match the chairs that circle around the stages, but in a tall, stool form, and on the edges of the room, the alcoves have been gutted and the couches have been replaced with black leather sectionals that fit to the walls and the same lights outline the small rooms, even curtains have been added to give the alcoves privacy. The girls sit around the main stage, while Jack leans against the stage, staring down at his phone.

"Legs, did you come to audition to be a dancer? We're full now, but you know I'll always make room for you." Leo smirks as he walks around the back of the bar, a water bottle in hand.

Huntley rolls her eyes. "No, I brought Reyna because fake Nox bailed on her and I wanted to see what you did to Second."

Leo's hazel eyes snap to mine. "You're hanging around with that lying piece of shit?" his tone is a little sharp, and it takes me back.

"I just need a ride, it's not that serious," I look between Huntley and Leo. They're both so fucking concerned about my life. It's irritating. I never wanted to be here in the first place.

Rolling my eyes, I turn and walk toward the stage, leaving them to do whatever the fuck they're doing.

"If you need a ride, I'll drive you," Leo calls behind me.

That stops me dead in my tracks, and the wheels in my brain turn. "Really? Whenever I need to go somewhere, no matter the time?" I ask, turning around.

Leo nods. "Yeah, just call me and I'll come get you."

Narrowing my eyes, I let them fall down his lean body. Long legs, wide shoulders, a trim waist. He's definitely hot. "Seems rather inconvenient."

He shrugs. "Better than a rat coming back into my clubhouse."

I run my tongue over my deep red lips and turn back around to join the other girls at the stage. Huntley says her goodbyes to Leo and Jack and leaves.

There's eleven of us girls here. Eight dancers—including me —two girls to work the bar, and the house mom, which I guess is similar to my responsibility at La Lujuria.

We go over the weekly schedule and the plan for Saturday— the reopening. I'm scheduled for Thursdays through Saturdays, from opening to whenever I want to leave. The club opens at nine, but they want us here by eight to get ready and be on the floor by the time customers arrive.

All is well—and boring, and the meeting is over quickly. They fill us in on their plans to open a liquor store next door and that they're going to start selling alcohol under the table in the club in the meantime. They're also upping security to be sure no one gets handsy with the girls.

We're dismissed and all make our way out of the club. I stop short once out the doors when I don't see Huntley's Jaguar parked where it was when we arrived; I should have expected that.

Someone traces the edge of my jeans, their finger trailing across my bare back between the gap of black cropped tee shirt and denim. "I told Huntley I'd drive you back to the clubhouse," Leo huskily says into my ear. I bite back the slight wave of interest his voice in my ear does to my body and keep my spine straight.

"Let's go then, pet." I remember the way his eyes burned when I called him that before.

He steps around me, the same glint in his eyes that I remember. Maybe it's annoyance or anger, maybe lust, hell it could be a combination of the three. "Have you ever been on the back of a bike?"

Smirking, I run my tongue between my lips. "I've ridden a lot of things before, but I can't say a motorcycle has been one."

He chuckles quietly, glancing over his shoulder briefly. "We'll get along just fine."

I follow Leo to his bike and watch as he slings his leg over, then glides the bike upright. He slips on a pair of dark sunglasses and turns to me.

And for the first time in my life, I admire a man. For more than his money or what he can do for me. But just because he looks really fucking good sitting on the powerful bike. His dark brown hair splays messily across his forehead, his hazel eyes reflecting the sunlight back to me, and one dimple pops out on his cheek as he smirks up at me. His soft, full lips contrast to his strong, straight nose and his sharp jaw.

He's very handsome.

There were good-looking men at the club. They weren't all shriveled up and popping Viagra like mints, but none of them looked like this.

Playful. Fun. Honest.

I wonder if I'll ruin that?

"You just put your foot on that peg and swing your leg over, Siren," his joking tone yanks me right out of my thoughts and plunges me back into the moment. "Here." He offers me his hand, and I take it. Following his instructions.

I sit on the way-too-small seat and place both feet on the tiny pegs. This doesn't seem safe.

"Hold on, baby. I promise to make your first time fun." I can hear the smirk in his voice even though I can't see it, and when he thumbs the button on the handlebar and the bike rumbles menacingly beneath me, I lurch forward, wrapping my arms around his tight, muscled abs.

He rolls out of the parking lot slowly, and I think this might not be too bad, but once the back tire hits the highway, Leo guns it, our bodies jerking with the harsh change of speed. A scream lodges in my throat as I cling to Leo tighter, my entire body pressing against his as closely as physically possible.

His loud laughter rises above the sound of the engine, but he slows down, one hand leaving the handlebars and resting against mine on his. "Did I scare you?"

"Yes!" I shriek.

His body shakes with what I realize is laughter and not the wind or the rumble of the bike. "You'll get used to it."

I want to smack him, but I get distracted by the trees whipping past us. They're so much more breathtaking in the open like this. The smell of the pines and the breeze blowing past us. I've never experienced anything like this.

I watch the trees the entire way back to the clubhouse, only realizing where we are when Leo slows to a stop to put in the code to the gate.

He drives me close to the door and stops, the bike's roar still loud but slightly quieter than before. He holds up his hand and I take it, climbing off the bike in a reverse way of the way I got on.

I try to pull my hand away, but he holds it tighter. When I meet his eyes, all the jokes from earlier are gone. "I'm serious, Reyna. No more rats. Call me when you need to go somewhere."

My brain must be recovering from the adrenaline from the ride, because I can't think of a snappy comeback, so I nod and finally he lets me pull my hand away.

My heart beats out of my chest as I walk to the door and the rumble of Leo's bike roars as he drives away. But I'm not sure if it's because of Leo or the ride.

Just out of curiosity, I walk through the main room slowly, my head swiveling back and forth. One door to Purgatory is open and the lights are off, so no one is in there.

The clubhouse has become so quiet without four prospects living here, or even without the entire club living here like we were a few weeks ago. Although, that was crowded as fuck and I'm glad to have my space again. But it's kind of sad to see the life that's left the clubhouse. The rowdy days where we just hung around and played pool or boxed in the ring outside.

I wonder if Jack will ever move out, or if we'll ever trust anyone else again to have prospects. Nox fucked us up good.

Anyway, no tattooed sirens down here, it seems, so I climb the familiar stairs two at a time and reach the top floor, making my way down the row of bedrooms until I come to Jack's. I bang on the door, letting him know I'm here and continuing a few more down to Mason's old room, or I guess still his room.

Glancing back at the door across from Mason's, I wait a moment to see if she'll open the door and peek out in the hallway at the commotion, but she doesn't, so I open the door

46

and walk inside to talk to Mason, leaving the door open for Jack, who should follow behind me soon.

"Miles give you a cool hacker name yet?" I ask instead of a hello and make my way to his bed, laying down at the foot with my legs still on the floor.

Mason sighs lightly. "You're not supposed to know about that." He stays focused on his screen.

"You shouldn't have told me then," I counter, staring at the popcorn ceiling. I don't know why people hate these so much. They're not bad, and who walks into a house and notices that sort of thing?

Jack walks in a moment later and closes the door behind him, pulling the stray chair away from Mason's desk and turning it sideways so he can face us both. He spreads his legs wide and leans down into the chair.

"So, have you looked into our new resident yet?" I ask Mason, putting my arms under my head to prop myself up a little.

"I'll start it now. Do you have her application?" Mase asks, turning around to glance at Jack and I.

Jack hands it to him and Mason looks it over. "Reyna Smith. Twenty-six from Seattle." He sets the paper down and starts working on his computers.

"Love Lies" by Khalid and Normani plays softly from Mason's computer speakers and I hum along to the tune.

"What if we call you Ghost?" I ask.

"Too overdone," Mason answers.

I hum to myself some more, thinking. "Ghost6969," I suggest again.

"Shut the fuck up," he laughs.

"Lord Overtron."

"I would literally rather die."

"Lord Overtron69."

"Please stop talking."

"Captain Computer." Mason and I go back and forth.

He shakes his head, his fingers flying like crazy over the keyboard. "I would rather go by what Miles calls me."

Sitting up, I ask, "What does he call you?"

Mason stays quiet for a moment, but finally says. "Floppy Dick." I nod my head, trying not to laugh.

"Floppy Dick69," Jack says from the corner, and Mason and I lose it. I'm doubled over laughing and Mason stops being a hacker genius to hide his face in his hands as he laughs loudly.

This is stupid and immature, but this is the most fun I've had with my brothers in months. We've attended so many funerals in the past few months, taken so many lives, and have fought so much. For each other, for this club, for our lives.

We haven't just sat and talked shit in so long. This is what we used to do when we first joined the club and everything was pussy and rainbows. My chest feels lighter being in here, laughing with my best friends.

"Shut up, assholes. I'm trying to work," Mason laughs, picking his head up and going back to his computer.

I lay my head back down, humming along to Mase's fire playlist as he works.

Finally, Mason sighs, "Goddamn it. This shit never fucking ends." He pushes away his keyboard and I dart up from the bed.

"What?" I ask, walking way too quickly than is necessary to look over his shoulder at his results. Not that I could tell a thing of what was on his screen.

"Reyna isn't who she says she is," Mason says, and Jack rolls toward us on his chair.

"What do you mean?" I ask, my heartbeat accelerating.

"I can't find any record of her. I didn't think I'd find any record of La Lujuria and her there, but there isn't a record of her working anywhere. The apartment she said she lived in wasn't rented by her. There isn't even a record of her being born. No social security number, no social media. Nothing."

"Fuck," I sigh, turning around and slumping onto the bed.

"We have to call Saint," Mason says, grabbing his phone from the desk.

"Yeah," I agree half heartedly. I don't know why I feel more crushed than angry. I was starting to feel something for Reyna, and now I don't even know who she is.

11

REYNA

 Huntley instructs.

I adjust my hips, holding up my fists with the heavy boxing gloves. Why did I agree to this? Probably because the blonde sadist just showed up at my door and told me we were coming to her studio to work out. She didn't give me a choice. I wish I could hit her instead of the bag.

Thwack! Thwack! Thwack! Sweat drips down my temple and my arms feel like lead.

"Okay, that's enough!" Huntley calls. My arms drop to my sides as my chest heaves. *Thank fuck.*

She hands me a black towel and water bottle as I pull on the velcro straps around my wrists and yank off the stupid gloves. I snatch the water bottle and unscrew the cap and take a long drink, grabbing the towel while chugging and wiping off the sweat between my tits.

"Did you have fun?" Huntley grabs the gloves off of the floor where I dropped them.

"No," I gasp, walking to the trash can by the door to throw away the empty water bottle. Huntley laughs while I swipe at the back of my neck with the sweat towel before tossing it in the bin next to the trash can. "You do that for fun?" I ask, falling to the black mat floor.

"I love kickboxing." Huntley smiles, sitting down next to me.

I shake my head. This woman is fucking crazy. "That was torture."

She laughs: a beautiful, sweet laugh, her white blonde hair swishes against the mats. "I did put you through a rougher routine, but I thought you were in shape." She smirks, and I want to wipe it off of her perfect fucking face.

"Fuck you, Lee." I drop to my back, trusting that she cleans this place thoroughly.

"Lee?" she chuckles.

I wave my hand in the air. "Your name is too long to say right now," I pant.

Her lips purse, but it slides into a smile. "I like it."

"Good." My breathing finally evens out, and my fear that my heart is going to explode lessens. "Because it was either that or bitch."

Huntley doubles over laughing, her hand slamming on the mat. "I suppose I could call you 'Ray', because you're such a ray of sunshine," she mocks me.

"If I'm your sunshine, I'd hate to see your darkness." I play along with her joke.

Huntley's blue eyes stare into my own and they make me feel vulnerable, like she might actually see me. "Why do you think you're so terrible? Just because you're not pink and frilly doesn't mean you're any less a good person."

I roll over onto my side, my black leggings hugging my hips and accentuating them. "Maybe you don't know me."

"Oh, that is definitely true, but I like you," she says.

My phone ringing from my bag interrupts Huntley's intrusive stare, and I drag it over by the strap and fish around for my phone.

Leo's name shines on the screen and I click 'answer.' "Hello?"

"Where the hell are you?" he snaps.

"Why are you keeping tabs on me?" I ask back, just as volatile.

"I thought we agreed I would drive you around," he says immediately.

"I'm with Huntley; I didn't run away." I roll my eyes.

There's a pause before his next question. "Where?"

Groaning, I shake my head. What the fuck is this? Am I back at La Lujuria? "Her torture studio, you stalker." Huntley laughs.

"I'm coming to pick you up," his voice is calm again, but it still holds a bit of a bite.

"Why?" I ask, annoyed.

"You're moving in with me." He hangs up, leaving that bomb hanging in the air.

12

LEO

Slam! Thunk. Thunk. Thunk. My heart beats in time with the heavy footfalls of my president as I wait for him.

Mase, Jack, and I sit around the chapel table silently, listening to the sound of Saint approaching.

I've barely taken my eyes off of the table, scenarios racing through my head. Why is she lying? What is she lying about? Who the fuck is she?

Saint steps into the room and I finally look up, following him through the room as he walks behind Mason and to his seat.

"Alright, what's going on? I'm between clients," Saint asks, sitting down and turning his chair to face us.

"I did that search on Reyna that you asked for," Mase starts.

"And?" Saint focuses on him. I notice he doesn't treat Mason any differently than he treats the rest of us when they're around the club. I thought he could have gotten a little more warmth from him since they share the same pussy, but I guess not.

"We don't know who she is. None of her story can be backed up." I listen as Mason fills Saint in. I can't speak. I don't want to speak.

"Her working at La Lujuria? The kidnapping?" Saint presses, his face setting into an icy glare.

Mason shakes his head. "La Lujuria didn't have security cams and I couldn't find any of their files. I think they were all destroyed, or maybe they kept paper logs. I don't know, but there isn't anything online for them." He sighs. "I couldn't find anything for when she was kidnapped. There isn't any indication that she and her boss escaped from La Lujuria, or that anyone ever found his body."

Saint runs his hands through his blonde hair, tousling his shoulder length hair with his fingers. "So a woman has been living in our clubhouse and getting close with our Old Ladies and we have no idea why she's here or who the fuck she is?" He sits back in his chair. His calm aura is the reason we all wanted him as our president when Ronan died. He always keeps a cool head—except when it comes to Allie. "What about Miles' girl? She used to work at La Lujuria. We can ask her if she knew Reyna, and at least get that part of her story confirmed."

Mason nods. "I'll call Miles."

"What do we do in the meantime?" I finally break my silence. This has been one of the burning questions running through my head. What will Saint do?

He shakes his head slowly. "I don't know. We've had so much shit happen to us, I'm half tempted to walk up to her room and put a bullet in her skull right now. I'd rather be safe than sorry."

Oh fuck. "Allie will divorce you before the ink is even dry on your marriage certificate, so how about we cool down and think of something else?" All eyes turn to me, and I know that I'm treading on thin ice.

"Hey, Miles," Mason interrupts me, *thank god,* and places his phone on the table in front of him.

"What do you want?" Miles sounds bored on the other end, his tone even and flat.

"We ended up taking in that girl that we saved from La Lujuria, and we want to check out her story and make sure she's who she says she is." Mason's eyes shift around the table.

"And what do you need from me?" he asks. Damn, he sounds worse than I feel right now.

"Uh," Mase bites his lips, pausing. "I was hoping you could ask Briar if she worked with a girl named Reyna. Black hair, tattoos, medium height."

"Briar's not here," Miles snaps, and we all exchange glances. Sighing, he continues, "She gave me a list of girls' names from the club that we looked for on the skin market. Let me check if she's on there." We wait with bated breath for Miles to tell us whether Reyna is who she says she is. "Yeah," he finally answers. "Reyna is on here. No last name. And we never found her."

"Did you find the other girls?" Jack asks, surprising me.

"Either them or their bodies," Miles answers evenly.

Mason and Miles hang up and the room goes quiet again. "Okay," I start. "So Reyna is indeed from the club, so what if..."

13

REYNA

"Excuse me?" My eyes widen, but a dial tone meets me on the other end. He fucking hung up on me.

Huntley packs her bag by the door, unaware of my conversation, and she turns to me, zipping her bag. "Do you want me to take you back to the clubhouse?"

I shake my head, still confused about what's going on. What prompted this sudden change? "No, Leo said he's coming to get me."

"Oh?" Huntley's arched brows raise. "I've never seen Leo put this much effort into a girl before."

"There's nothing going on there." I roll my eyes, shaking my head again.

"Yes, there is." She smirks. "Leo has never done anything for a girl unless he's friends with them, and I'm his only friend."

"I'm sure he's just trying to sleep with me," I say, annoyed.

Huntley laughs, dropping her bag to the floor and coming to sit next to me again. "Oh, he's definitely trying to sleep with you, but it's more than that. I can see it in his eyes."

Me too, I think. He's obvious. It's written all over his body, and

I might let him. He's attractive. Why not have some fun before I go?

'Before I go'. My stomach clenches at the thought of leaving Huntley, the first person I've ever liked enough to call a friend—even though it's still too early to be real friends—and even leaving Leo makes me a little sad. This is so new to me: building meaningful relationships.

Huntley's little guard dog stirs in the corner, rising to sit, her attentive eyes focused on the door. I completely forgot she was here. She was so quiet through our torture session.

Leo steps inside and the dog stares at him a moment before she hurries over and brushes against his leg. He bends down to kiss her nose and scratch her ears. "Hey, sweet girl, were you watching over mama?" he coos, and I have to admit, something small in me stirs, but I push it down, ignoring it.

His hazel eyes fall on me, running down my body. My exposed stomach, and down my legging-clad legs.

I set my arms on the floor behind me, subtly pushing my chest out in my black, low cut sports bra.

Leo drags his hand through his dark brown hair, looking away. "Come on, Siren." With a heavy breath, he turns, "See ya, Legs!" he calls over his shoulder and opens the door.

"Bye," she says, and I don't miss the smirk plastered on Huntley's face.

I push off of the floor, refusing to turn around and look at her gloating face. Noctem eyes me as I pass, and I open the door and step out into the crisp fall air. It's not quite cold yet, but it's cooling down every day, the summer air fading, the light warm breeze that carries the fresh salt water in from the Sound. Now, the scent of pine needles and crisp rain fills the air.

Leo is leaning against his black mustang, his tanned arms crossed in front of his body, staring straight ahead into the open grassy area that surrounds Evan's Body Shop and Huntley's little studio.

"What's going on, Leo?" I snap, walking toward him, crossing my own arms as I stop next to him.

"You're moving in with me," he states plainly.

I glare at him. He's so infuriating sometimes. What the fuck is going on? How do they just decide where I go, like some piece of furniture? "Why are you moving me out of the clubhouse, and why do I have to move in with you? If the club doesn't want me there anymore, I'll just find my own place."

Leo finally turns to me, his head snapping in my direction. "The club promised to take care of you, and we're going to do that, but you just can't live at the clubhouse anymore. Saint doesn't want anyone there except for members."

"What about—" I start to ask.

"I'm your only option. Everyone else is married. Look. it won't be that bad. I have my own house, you'll have your own room, but we'll have to share a bathroom while I'm renovating mine. It's private, it's safe. You'll be fine there."

I realize that there isn't any other option here besides leaving completely, and I can't do that yet, so I end the conversation with an eye roll and try to reach behind Leo for the door handle.

He swivels around, grabbing the handle, and opens the door for me. With his back to me, I drag my long nail along his waist, over his shirt as I step around him. His head turns, and he watches me walk around him. I hold his gaze as I bend and slide into the car.

I can feel the tension between us, and I know exactly what's going to happen when we're stuck in the same place together.

———

Leo waited at the bar while I packed my things, which were just my clothes, toiletries, and bedding. He helped me carry out my suitcase and a basket and we drove through Merrill Hill and out the other end in silence. I kept waiting for him to turn into some residential area, but he drove past them all. The further away the little town gets, the more anxious I become. Where is he taking me?

Leo turns down a dirt road, thick trees lining both sides. "Are you bringing me out here to kill me?" I add a joking tone to the question to hide my genuine fear.

Silence stretches out between us, making my palms sweat against my leggings. "Is there a reason I should kill you?" he asks, his eyes forward and his foot pressing gently on the brake. He takes a wide curve and the trees open up to a large clearing with a medium-sized cabin sitting in the middle. The lawn is kept and there's a large pond in front of the house. Leo parks next to his bike and gets out.

Taking a deep breath, I push open the door and step out. "Is this your house?" I ask, stepping around the back of the vehicle where Leo is opening the trunk. I can't help but ask questions. It really does feel like he's about to murder me out here.

"What else would it be?" He slams the trunk closed, holding both my bag and the basket holding my bedding.

He walks away, not waiting for me to reply, and I follow behind him cautiously, my head swiveling around to survey everything.

Thick woods surround the cabin, and it's absolutely silent out here.

We walk around the side of the cabin, to the front, and I follow Leo onto the wide porch. Two rocking chairs sit in front of the large window, looking out at the pond. It's quite nice actually, and I'm sure I'd be able to appreciate it more, if I weren't on edge about what will be on the other side of the door.

Leo maneuvers the basket in his hands around, reaching into his pocket for the key, I'm assuming, so I take the opportunity to subtly look through the window and into the cabin. Practically, the entire front wall of the cabin is a window, so it's easy. It looks empty.

He gets the door unlocked and pushes it open, stepping inside.

"Welcome home, Siren." He turns around, smirking and walking backward through the living room.

14

REYNA

The cabin isn't that bad. It's rather small and rustic, but it's nice.

Everything is wood, the walls, the floors, the ceiling. The only materials that aren't wood are the soft leather couch and chairs, the plain, matte black counters atop the matte olive green cabinets, and the stainless steel appliances. However, the upper cabinets in the kitchen? Wood.

Looking around, I follow Leo around the couch and down a narrow hallway. All the walls are bare, no art or pictures hang anywhere. The home looks like what I would expect Leo to live in. Basic and masculine. Like he really only put thought into the furniture.

He pushes open the door on the right and walks through. This room is even more plain than my room at the clubhouse. A bed, dresser, and a small closet.

Leo sets my bags and basket on the carpeted floor and turns around to face me. "Bathroom is next door and my room is in the loft upstairs." He looks around the room, then back at me. "Are you hungry?"

"Are you going to feed me after uprooting my life? How

kind." I cross my arms over my chest and stare at him. His excuse to make me move was weak, and I don't believe it.

Leo's eyes narrow, and I watch him intently. I've never seen this expression on him before. "We took you in when you needed protection. Maybe show some fucking respect, Reyna," he snaps, his hazel eyes blazing.

"I gave your club information that you failed to find on your own." I seethe back at him. I may keep to myself a lot, but one thing Leo will learn about me now is that no man will ever scare me, and I will always speak my mind and defend myself.

He chuckles coldly, his eyes roaming down my body, but not in his playful or familiar lustful way. It feels like he's sizing me up, assessing me. "It wouldn't be the first time we got information and disposed of the messenger working for the enemy."

And there it is.

The club doesn't trust me.

I had anticipated this. They would be fools to let me into their home without an ounce of distrust, but they're also men, and when they see a vulnerable, scared woman, they can't help but lend a hand, even if that hand leads to their demise.

That's something that women had to learn a long fucking time ago. Always expect the hand that helps you to close around your throat the minute they've lifted you up.

Leo storms out of the room, taking his surly cloud with him. It doesn't bother me any.

Cabinets open and close loudly in the kitchen while I unpack my clothes, placing them in the dresser and closet. I finish making the bed with my bedding—excuse me for not trusting Leo's housekeeping skills—and leave my room.

Leo pulls a pizza from the oven and sets it on a large cutting board on the stove.

"Did you just make that?" I lean over the peninsula counter and watch him cut the pizza into slices.

He looks over his shoulder at me briefly before focusing on the pizza again. "It's a frozen pizza."

"I've never had a frozen pizza before." I lean to the side to see around him, eyeing the pizza. It looks good.

Leo places slices on two plates and turns around, setting the plates between us on the counter. "You've never had a frozen pizza before?" he asks, his eyes narrowing slightly.

I shrug, picking up a slice from my plate. Gooey cheese strings trail off of the slice and steam rises to my nose and fills it with the mouthwatering aroma. Now would be a good time to be honest with Leo. Or a terrible time. But I know this is for the best. "I lied about living in an apartment in Seattle. I actually lived on Martin Island at the club, and hardly ever left the island."

No shock or questioning pass over Leo's face, so I know he knew something and was waiting to either catch me in a lie or for me to confess. I was right. I needed to say something today. "Why did you lie?"

"I was afraid you would think I did more than just work for La Lujuria. I knew a lot of inside information, but I never did more than just work there. What Los Lobos had going on was all them."

Leo's eyes never leave my own. The playful warmth that normally exudes from them is gone though, this is the man in the outlaw biker gang. "Where did I take you the night we rescued you?"

Jesus, I should have expected an interrogation after I started admitting, so I set my pizza down. This isn't going to end anytime soon. "My boss, Hector's apartment. He was already dead by that time. That's where the Kings kidnapped me from and took me back to La Lujuria."

"What happened at La Lujuria?" he asks.

My mind drifts back to that evening. The chaos, the screaming, the gunshots, and blood. I stare at the black countertop and answer as detached from the memory as I can. It was the first time I ever felt actual fear. "Men stormed the club right before opening. They beat the few clients that we had unconscious. They killed our security and the few Los Lobos that were there. Shot them, cut their throats, cut open their stomachs and left them to bleed out on the floor. It was—"

I cringe at the memory, swallowing hard. "It was like the worst of mankind come to life. I recognized some of the men as Lobos, but a lot of them I had never seen before. While some men were killing all the men who worked at the club, others were grabbing the women. Dragging them by their hair, punching them in the face and knocking them unconscious. Hector and I were in the kitchen. I was late in finishing my meal when we heard the screams and gunshots, and we watched what was happening on the security monitor." I want to look up at Leo, to maybe see if I can tell what he's thinking while I recount the worst moment of my life, but I keep my eyes on the counter, so I continue. "Hector sprung into action. He knew they would kill him and take me, so we snuck out of the kitchen and through a part of the club that the guys had already made their way through. I slipped in the blood, and Hector had to hold my hand to keep me upright. We went through a side door and escaped in a helicopter. A man chased us. My heels caught on a loose brick while running, and I nearly broke an ankle. Hector was shot in the shoulder, but we made it off of the island and back to his apartment. We were supposed to lie low until we could get out of the country, but the Kings found us before that."

"You should have told us that in the beginning," Leo says, but his voice has softened slightly from before.

Now I finally do glance up at him, and I glare. How dare he tell me how I should have reacted when he's never had to live with the fear of what I went through. "I didn't know who the

Kings were at that point, and I didn't know who you were. I was just trying to stay alive; that's all I've been doing since Hector and I left Martin Island." So much truth spills out in that last sentence, that goosebumps rise on my arms.

Silence stretches between us for a long time before Leo speaks up again. "What's your real name?"

I narrow my eyes. "Reyna."

He purses his lips and shakes his head. "You're lying."

If I was sitting, I would push off of my chair. I'm so upset. "I'm not lying. That's the truth."

Leo leans across the counter, his face coming closer to mine. "We can't find any record of you existing anywhere. No birth certificate, no social, no death cert. So what is your real name or who erased you and why?"

He knows more than I gave him credit for.

I lick my lips to give myself a moment to collect myself. I didn't expect Leo to look so far into me. "My name is Reyna, or at least that's what the club had always called me. I came to the club when I was really young, and I don't remember my life before."

"What do you mean?" Leo interrupts me.

"I mean, I only know what I've been told." I snap. "Hector's dad found me when I was little and took me to the club, and they raised me there. I had a nanny until I could stay on my own, and then I lived on the island by myself full time. When I was underage, I worked in the office, then when I became of age, I moved into the entertainment side. Hector and I were kind of raised together, and he took over the club when his dad stepped down." I pause, trying to remember my earliest memories. "Hector's dad said I looked like a princess, but the man who owned La Lujuria said I looked like a queen. He only spoke Spanish, so they started calling me Reina, the Spanish word for queen. I adapted it to Reyna."

Leo lets out a long breath, and I watch him. I unloaded a lot just now. "Who owns the club? I thought Los Lobos owned it?"

I shrug. "I don't know. Hector would never tell me, but he wasn't part of Los Lobos."

The fire in his eyes is finally gone. "You don't remember anything?"

Shaking my head, my eyes drift to the ceiling. "I only remember walking up the steps to La Lujuria for the first time, and even that is hazy."

Leo looks down and sighs, "At least the pizza has cooled down now."

15

LEO

MY FOOT BOUNCES WHERE IT'S PROPPED AGAINST MY KNEE. I TOLD
Reyna to be ready by four so we could go to club dinner at
Saint's, but it's now five past four, and she's still fucking around
in her room while I wait for her in the living room.

Fucking finally, the door at the end of the hall clicks open
and I hear the thunk of her heels on the hardwood floor.

Standing up, I drag my hands down my jeans, getting ready
to rip into her for being late, but as fucking always, my mouth
dries up and my throat closes at the sight of her, skintight, black,
distresses skinny jeans, a black crop top that shows off a thin
sliver of stomach and her round tits, and a black leather jacket.
Her raven hair hangs in a long curtain down her back and her
dark red lips look pouty as she stares at me.

"Are we going to go, or are you just going to stare at me all
day?" she sasses, and it pulls me out of my stupor. Fuck, this
woman can always read my goddamn mind, and I hate it.

Frustrated, I pick up the store bought potato salad and turn
away from her, heading for the door and letting her follow
along.

The trees are changing their colors, and I'm excited to see

the bright oranges and yellows mixing with the deep green evergreens that surround my cabin.

Tonight's club dinner is to celebrate the reopening of the Second Circle. Our opening night is tomorrow, and to be frank, I'm really proud of Jack and I. This is the first thing that we're really in charge of for the club, and if this goes well, it won't only benefit us but all our brothers as well. Which is a huge incentive. But it also means that if we shit the bed, the entire club suffers as well.

Opening my saddle bag on my bike, I put the container of potato salad in and shut the lid. I swing my leg over the seat and sit down, raising the handlebars and putting the bike upright.

A small smile pulls at Reyna's full lips before she sucks them between her teeth to hide it. She enjoys being on the bike. Good.

She climbs on like a pro and wraps her leather clad arms around my waist, her chin resting on my cut over my shoulder. Her musky, cherry scent wafts over me and warmth settles in my stomach, and it scares me. Since when do I allow women on the back of my bike? Since when do I get "warm, fuzzy feelings" like some romance movie? Maybe I'm coming down with something.

Every once in a while, I glance in my small mirror to check on Reyna. Her head is on a constant swivel, like she's seeing the world for the first time, and I guess if her story had any truth to it last night, she kind of is. She said she didn't leave the island much, and so I guess she never got to see the Sound from this side. She never got to see the view from Orca Bay: the line of mountains on the other side of the water.

Three bikes sit in a line in Saint's driveway, and it feels like a punch to the gut. This is all that's left of the Devil's Outlaws Washington chapter: the six of us. We lost four great brothers and a rat prospect, all in only a few months' time.

I park my bike next to Cale's and Reyna lets go and steps off of the bike, her cherry scent pulling away with her and finally giving me a chance to breathe regular air. Air that's not suffocating me with the most beautiful woman I've ever seen.

Jesus Christ, I'm fucked.

We're silent as we walk to the front door and let ourselves in. Voices and "Blastoff" by Internet Money drift through the Viotto house, saying all of their names is just too damn long.

Brothers and their girls are scattered throughout the open plan house. Reese is putting trays of desserts in the fridge that Allie is holding open for her while Cale places another few trays on the stove. Saint and Jack are sitting at the long outdoor table talking quietly and watching Finn and Randy at the smoker. Finn throws his head back and his laugh echoes, probably all the to the water. Huntley walks down the hall, presumably from the bathroom, wringing her hands together. And Mason is making her dad a drink at the new outdoor kitchen on the back porch.

Allie and Reese say hello to me as I pass them and Cale gives me a nod. Allie smiles at Reyna behind me, but I don't miss the slight glare Reese gives her.

Actually, if I'm being honest, my hackles raise at the sight of it, and it pisses me off. I love Reese. She's an Old Lady, but I thought marrying Cale and getting deeper in club life taught her to not be judgmental anymore. I don't know, maybe I'm looking too far into it. Maybe there's no glare and I'm just making shit up. Maybe she's having a bad day. That would make sense with what she and Cale are going through right now. That would also explain the six trays of desserts she brought. She is a stress baker, after all.

But I hate Reyna is making me feel this shit. Protective and looking into fucking glances from the Old Lady's. Like, what the fuck? I've never cared about shit like this before, but now I don't want Reese's side eye to offend Reyna.

Huntley and Reyna walk together outside, and I push my

thoughts aside. If there's one thing I can do well, it's compartmentalize. I'll worry about that shit later.

"Hey, can we talk?" I lean over the outdoor kitchen counter as Huntley's dad, Nik, takes the glass from Mason and leaves, smiling at me as he goes.

"Yeah." Mason screws the cap onto a bottle of liquor, waiting for me.

I shake my head. "Not here," I say, a little quieter.

Mason nods and steps around the island, and I follow him to the garage.

I shut the door behind me and he crosses his arms, standing in the middle of the full garage. I guess Saint wasn't planning on sharing his Old Lady with another man when he bought the house. They're running out of space in here with two bikes and Saint and Allie's Audis. They kicked Mase's poor truck out to the driveway.

"I got some information about Reyna." I join him in front of Allie's car, standing close to him.

"Great, but why did you need to tell me instead of telling the entire club?"

I bite the inside of my lip. I kind of am going behind the club's back, but it's for a good reason. "I didn't want to wait, and I need you to fact check it before I bring it to the club as truth."

Mason nods. "Okay, what's her story?"

It feels like I have a lead ball in my stomach as I prepare to tell Mason everything Reyna told me last night, like I'm betraying her, but she had to know I'd tell the club, right? And my alliance is with the club before her. "She doesn't know. The previous manager of La Lujuria picked her up off of the street and she doesn't remember anything before going to the club. She doesn't know her real name. Reyna is the name the club gave her. She's been living completely at the club since she got there when she was little." Saying all of that sounds even crazier than when she told me, and I can tell Mason is just as puzzled as I am.

"What the fuck?" he finally says.

"Yeah," I agree, pursing my lips in a 'told you so' kind of way.

He sighs, and I can see the wheels turning in his big brain. "So we have no idea who she is and no way to find out. She knows absolutely nothing?"

"Correct." I nod.

He narrows his eyes at me. "She's got to be lying."

I shrug. I've been thinking about this all night. "I don't know. It sounds far-fetched, but it makes sense."

Mason shakes his head. "Fine, then get some DNA from her and bring it to me. I'll have it run and we can figure out who she is or who she's related to."

"How am I supposed to get that?" I ask, my brows pulling down over my eyes.

Mason walks toward the door leading into the house. "I don't know," he calls over his shoulder, turning slightly to look at me. "She lives with you now, right? Get creative."

The door closes behind him and once again I'm left alone with thoughts of Reyna, but this time they're a lot less entertaining.

———

WE ALL SIT around the long wood table on the wide back porch, plates of food empty and the light thrum of conversation fills the evening air. String lights line the ceiling outside along with an outdoor light fixture and it's incredibly peaceful.

Good food, great company, and a fantastic fucking view. What more could a guy ask for?

Saint clears his throat and pushes away from the table. Everyone's eyes snap to him as he walks to the outdoor kitchen and grabs a box from the counter. "We should have done this months ago when you three were patched into the club, but a lot of shit happened and we were too busy celebrating weddings and putting brothers into the ground, so I hope you'll forgive me for forgetting." He walks to stand behind Allie and places his hand on her shoulder. He hands Mason a small, black, velvet bag and then walks around the table and hands one to Jack and I. "These are Gremlin Bells." I open the bag and pull out a small metal bell, smaller than my palm. The Outlaw skull is etched onto it, with the top rocker like on our cuts, our names below where the state rocker normally is. "You put this on your bike and it's supposed to keep you safe on your travels and bring you good luck. I'd say you've all fared quite well this long without it, but I don't want to take any chances."

The bell clatters as I turn it, the clapper inside smacking against the chrome.

"I didn't think you were superstitious." Mase grins from the other side of Allie as Saint takes his seat.

Saint stares at the table. "Ronan gave all of us our bells. It was time I give you yours. And maybe it's complete bullshit, but ours have kept us safe while on the road, and it's tradition, so put it on your fucking bike."

Allie runs her hand down Saint's arm and he looks at her, his hard features softening as he stares into her eyes, her lips lifted in a small smile.

Turning my head, I catch Reyna already looking at me, and for maybe the first time her eyes aren't guarded and I see actual emotion in them. But before I can figure out what she's feeling, her face freezes over and the mask is back, shielding whatever I thought I just saw.

16

REYNA

—staying up all night and sleeping through the day—I just kept myself awake by binging a fairy show, which was great until they canceled it after only two seasons. It did what it needed to do, though, and I finally went to sleep in the early morning hours, sleeping until midday.

I heard Leo keeping himself awake in the living room with some game where he had to shoot a lot of people. I could hear him groaning—presumably when he died—but he kept himself rather quiet. I didn't dare leave my room. Not after dinner yesterday.

I let myself have one weak moment, where I thought about what it would feel like to comfort someone I loved, and Leo caught me. I can't let that happen again.

Anyway, it doesn't matter. I'm here for one reason and one reason only: to survive and get answers.

I pack my duffle with makeup and hair products and my outfit and heels for tonight. I set the bag on the floor, and open my door to go to the restroom to shower.

Opening the door, I stop in my tracks when I come face to face with a naked Leo.

Steam billows out of the bathroom behind him and water trails down his tan chest and through the valley of his abs, right down to the towel wrapped loosely around his narrow hips.

My eyes slowly trace back up his body and find his eyes already watching me, a playful smirk forming on his beautiful face.

He leans forward, the heat of his body wafting off of him and wrapping around me like a warm blanket, the scent of his clean body wash filling my nose. "I left some hot water for you." He pulls away as quickly as he came and walks down the hall, his wide back mocking me as he goes.

I hurry into the bathroom and lock the door behind me. Why does he make me feel these things that I haven't felt in so long? Tingles of anticipation and excitement ignite through my body, but I duck under the stream and douse them in cold water.

———

SECOND CIRCLE IS in full buzz. Girls hurry around the locker room, curling their hair, applying makeup, and exchanging their comfortable sweats for barely there lingerie. The front of the club is just as busy. The bartenders are getting their station in order. Leo and Jack go back and forth, making sure everyone has everything they need, but I notice how Leo steers clear of me, choosing to stand in the doorway and avoid eye contact when he comes back to the locker room.

I straighten my hair, and apply my thick winged liner along with a deep red matte lipstick, and change into my costume. A see through bra, with flesh toned mesh and black snakes over the cups. My nipples peep through the mesh material, and the underwear is similar but with a black panel covering what legally can't be seen in the club. I strap on my black heels to complete the look and brush my hair out one more time.

I'm the opener tonight—and every night that I'm scheduled. Most of the girls are nervous, probably because it's their first time, but not me. I've danced in front of other people a thousand times. This isn't anything new, or I guess it somewhat is: I won't have to fuck anyone for money after I dance.

Looking around, I watch the girls. Some of them chat with one another, others sit quietly as they work on themselves or mess around on their phones. I won't be getting close to these girls, much like I never got close to any of the girls I worked with before. At the end of the day, they're competition and I like to win.

"Reyna, you're up!" Stephanie, the house mom, calls, walking through the door from the front of the club. I stand and walk with confidence toward the door, keeping my head high. "It's packed out there! The most I've ever seen in a night!" She smiles wide, and I know she's excited for her cut of our pay.

Learning the strip club payout method has been truly fucked. We have to pay the club for coming in, tip the DJ, the bar staff, security, and the house mom from whatever we make each night. At least at La Lujuria, the club never took a cut of our earnings. The guests had to pay up front to get in and then they paid us after our service. We didn't have to tip the bodyguards or the kitchen staff.

Stephanie was right. The club is packed. People line the bar and the stage, some even have to stand because there aren't enough seats. The plan is, I'm going to dance on the main stage alone, and then after me, three girls will work the three stages at the same time for short segments of songs, in between, each girl gets to do one solo dance to an entire song. In total, I'm dancing three times tonight. Two solo and one group dance.

A security guard leads me through the throng of people and

to the stage. The lights are low, and when I step up to the stage, the LEDs turn from blue to red, and all chatter stops.

"Unholy" by Sam Smith and Kim Petra thumps through the club as I take the steps one at a time to the beat of the song. I drop to my knees, grabbing onto the pole and popping my ass and then bending backwards, facing the crowd, keeping my face relaxed with a sultry gaze. Money slowly falls onto the stage, and it is a different sight to see. Normally, my customers just enjoyed my dancing for free. I push forward and turn around, placing my hands and chest on the stage, bouncing my ass in the air, and then dropping it from side to side onto the stage.

The rush of adrenaline pulses through my body, making me feel alive, and I eat it up. I love this feeling. The feeling of holding people captive with my body, their entire attention unwavering on me.

I roll over onto my back, moving my hands down my body and then pushing up to sit. I face the side, to give the audience on the other side a view, and open my legs wide and toss my head back in unison with the *ding* in the song. Rolling to my knees, I whip my hair around, feeling it brush across my hands on the stage, and move to my knees again. I crawl to the pole and run my hands up it to make sure it isn't slick, moving to the music, so it looks like part of the dance. Standing, I get a good grip, and when the beat drops, I swing my body around dramatically, snapping my legs wide as my back hits the pole and then closing them and spinning around. I place my feet onto the floor for a brief moment, using the momentum to toss my body into a back tuck, landing in the splits on the stage.

The crowd cheers and some gasp as I lean forward, bending my back leg and then bringing them together and rolling out of my splits and onto my stomach. I rise onto my knees and smooth my hands down my body before grabbing onto the pole again and spinning around once with my legs tucked into my body. Bills rain down onto the stage, covering it almost completely.

For a moment, I make eye contact with Leo. He's standing at the bar surrounded by the rest of the club, but I don't focus on them, only him.

I lick my lips, staring right at him and invert, turning my body upside down and doing straddle waves with my legs. Hooking one leg around the pole, I slide down until my back hits the stage, and I slide off, never taking my eyes off of Leo's.

His body looks tight with tension as I roll mine to the beat of the song, thrusting my hips in the air.

Turning over, I climb to my feet with my hand on the pole and climb it, before inverting again and letting go, spinning quickly as I reach behind me and unhook my bra, holding onto it with one hand and dropping it to the stage in the pile of money.

Manly cheers erupt from the crowd, and I force myself not to roll my eyes at their immaturity. Leo doesn't cheer though, he just stares right at me. His eyes go wide and his chest rises rapidly.

I take hold of the pole again and pull myself up, dropping one leg and letting my legs fall into the splits as I hold one of them against the pole.

Turning my back, I slide the pole between my legs and press my chest out, spinning around with my hands wrapped around the pole above me.

I let go of the pole and fall forward, placing my hands on the ground and then kicking off of the pole, dropping my legs behind me in a bridge. As soon as the toe of my heels hit the stage, I push off of them and do a kick over, pausing in the splits in the air before dropping onto my knees on the floor.

More cheers and whoops, money lightly falls onto me as I close my eyes and rest my hands on my thighs, dropping my hand back and letting my hair sweep across my lower back as the song fades to a close.

Guards come to the stage and help me sweep up my money and place it into a bag. I pick up my bra in between my fingers and smile flirtatiously at the people surrounding the stage.

Leo meets me at the bottom of the stairs, holding his hand out for me to use to get down.

His hand is feverish on my skin as he places it on my lower back and leads me through the crowd and towards the back room.

"You're not doing lap dances during your group dance," he says, his voice stern.

17

REYNA

"Oh my god, you killed that!" Huntley gushes, sliding up next to me and grabbing my arm. She looks exquisite in her distressed boyfriend jeans and white crop top. "Can I buy a dance from you?" She smirks, raising her brows conspiratorially.

We reach the locker room, and I pull her in with me, leaving Leo at the door. "I have a better idea. How about you do a dance with me next weekend?" I take the bag of money to my locker.

"Oh." Her heels click on the tile floor behind me. "I don't know about that. I'm not sure how Finn would feel and he's the only person I've ever danced for."

Shrugging, I shove my bag into my locker and lock it. "That's sweet, but the offers always there. I think you'd have fun. There's nothing better than the cheers from the stage."

Huntley purses her red lips, her already high cheekbones popping. "Your dance did make me wonder what it was like. Everyone went crazy for you."

I slide my bra straps up my arms. "You don't have to strip. We can just do a routine together. We can wear costumes and you can wear a mask if you really want to have some anonymity."

She smiles and nods. "Okay, let's do it!"

I hook the back of my bra. "Okay, we can get together and choreograph something, but I have to go find Leo and figure out what's going on."

Huntley says goodbye and we part ways at the locker room door. I have to shove my way through the crowd in search of Leo. It really is packed in here, and multiple people stop me to ask when I'm dancing next or if they can buy a dance.

Leo is nowhere in sight, so I stop at the bar and ask Jack. "Where's Leo? I need to speak with him." I shout over the music.

Jack looks around while cleaning a short tumbler. "Check the office," he says.

I turn around without another word and head for the hallway at the side of the building.

There are three doors down this hallway: one to the office, another to a storage room, and the last is a back exit.

Pushing open the door, I find Leo slouched behind the desk with a glass in his hand.

He cocks his head. "Shouldn't you have knocked? This is your boss's office."

"I don't really care." I take the seat across from him and glance down at the paperwork spread out on the desk. He chuckles and takes a sip of the amber liquid. "Why can't I give dances during the group dance?"

His hazel gaze burns into my skin as he stares at me, but I kind of like it. It's warm. Not cool and calculating like all of the times people have looked at me before. Excited about what I'm going to do for them or what they get to do to me. "I don't think it'll be safe."

"That's a lie. I just walked through the club and not a single person so much as bumped my shoulder. This is the safest place because every person in here knows if they cross a stripper, they are crossing your club." I cross my arms under my tits, pressing them up.

Leo's eyes flash down briefly before meeting my eyes again. "Okay, you're right."

"I know I am." I push off of the chair and stand, smirking down at Leo's open mouth. I don't think he's used to being called out on his shit. Well, he better get used to it.

"Hey, before you go," Leo calls as I reach the door to leave.

"What?" I turn around and drop my head to the side.

His narrowed eyes set me on edge, but I keep my outward cool. He's Outlaw Leo right now. "Did you work with a girl named Briar at La Lujuria?"

I blink once, then twice. Why is he asking about Briar? "Yeah," I answer. Did something happen to Briar? I mean, I *know* something happened to her. I know all the girls were kidnapped and sold into something horrendous, but I know nothing beyond that. Maybe Briar was found, maybe she escaped like me.

"What does she look like?" he asks, his tone even. This is a test. He knows Briar.

I smirk, but cover it by licking my lips, which Leo can't help but watch. "She's short. Brunette with huge green eyes that she never grew into. She has a nice rack though, but so did everyone at La Lujuria. We had the best plastic surgeons as our clients." Leo nods and turns back to the papers sitting in front of him, but I can't leave just yet. "Is she okay?" I ask.

Leo looks up again and sighs. "She escaped, not long after you did, I assume. She's with a friend of the club."

That's enough for me, so I turn around and step out of the office.

"Do you care about the other girls? About what happened to them?" he calls after me.

Halting in my tracks, I stare at the ground for a long moment. "It's easier not to," I say over my shoulder and leave before he can ask me anything else.

Was I friends with the women I worked with? No. Did I want them to be killed and trafficked? Never in a million years. I may not have been their friend, but I still looked after them and knew almost everything about them. Some of them were saving up to start a career, others were using the club as a way to pay for school, others just enjoyed the money. It didn't matter the reason they were doing sex work; they were still humans, and they didn't deserve what happened to them.

But still saying all of that, it's easier if I don't think about them, because what the fuck can I do to save any of them? I have no idea where they were sent and where they are now. I just hope that they are either dead or saved.

18.

LEO

Short, petite girl with big green eyes. That's how Mason described Briar. He left out her great rack, but I'd bet he probably wasn't looking with his whipped ass. Reyna described her in the same way, so I trust that she really did work at La Lujuria. It gives me hope if she wasn't lying about that.

I glance down at the liquor store expansion before bunching the papers together in a stack and leaving the office.

The bass thumps so loudly in the club that I can feel it in my chest. Reyna fucking killed it tonight on stage. I'm not a stranger to a strip club—certainly not Second Circle—and I've never seen so many people captivated by one dancer. The entire club was focused on her and only her.

She had to have made over a grand just in that once dance. Honestly, it was probably closer to three.

That's insane for our club. We aren't a big club; we aren't in a big city. The Second Circle is a decent sized club in a small city. Girls are making hundreds a night, maybe a grand on good nights, but never in one dance, and a stage dance at that. Normally, our girls make the majority of their money during private dances or party rooms.

A few more girls come out to the stage for their dances—none of them even coming close to Reyna's dance—and I help at the bar, getting girls for their dances, and hanging with my brothers. We're only halfway through the night, and it's been a very successful night. Jack and I are happy. Actually, I'm thrilled. I've had jobs before, but I've never been in charge of anything. I'm proud of us and I'm proud of all the girls. They all look great and I can tell they have been practicing their routines.

Saint stops me as I walk past him. "You did good tonight. Keep this up and you might be the most profitable Outlaw business." He pats me on the shoulder, a happy, tipsy smile plastered on his face. It's really good to see him smile again.

I nod my thanks and move along, taking a drink to a customer at the stage.

The music changes and girls step onto the stages around the club, Reyna on the main stage and two other dancers at the other poles. It's time for the group dance. The blue LEDs turn purple and the dancers all take the stage, doing their own dance to the same song. But I'm focused on Reyna as she spins around the pole, already topless, her pink nipples hardened.

I'm instantly hard, which is quite embarrassing. But I'm captive to her, standing in the same spot, watching her body with fascination. She's like a siren, calling me with her body and holding me immobile.

She does more incredibly impressive pole moves before she drops to the floor and crawls to the edge of the stage, her ass moving side to side in her dark thong.

Her narrowed eyes hold mine. If sex could be a person, it would be Reyna. Everything about her is sensual. The way she looks, moves, and smells.

My eyes widen as she climbs off the stage and walks to a man sitting in a chair next to me. The same customer I just brought a drink.

This bitch.

She sets her legs on either side of his hips and sits in his lap, facing him. She moves her hips in a circle over his dick, her tits almost brush his face as her body moves.

My blood boils as I watch her move. I told her not to give a lap dance, didn't I? I know I didn't imagine that.

Stepping forward, I grab her wrist and pull her off of him. Her bare breasts press into my shirt and I gulp.

"Can I help you?" she asks, her dark red lips parted seductively.

"Didn't I tell you no lap dances?" I snarl, ignoring her lips and tits. Goddamn, she's fucking perfect.

Her head cocks to the side and she runs her blue eyes down my chest to where we're touching and then back up. "What makes you think you can tell me what I can and cannot do, pet?" She yanks her wrist out of my tight grip and turns her back to me.

Reyna lifts one leg over one guy and gyrates more, then swings her body around and sits on his lap with her back to him. Her head turns, and she watches me as she dances on him. His eyes are wide as he stares at her ass and I want to kill her.

But I also want to fuck her.

Which is fucking confusing and toxic as all hell. But I've never had a woman turn me down or defy me. I mean, I've never cared enough to tell a woman to do anything, and here I am. Is this jealousy? I want to gouge the man's eyes out, but he did nothing wrong. Just in the right place at the right time.

He's definitely going to go home and jack himself to the memory of Reyna's tits in his face.

Fuck, I might too.

The dance ends after what feels nine years, and Reyna finally leaves the fucking sap and looks away from me, letting a guard escort her back to the locker room while another one cleans up the money from her stage. Looking around, I notice that the other girls barely have any money on their stages. I hadn't realized before, but most of the patrons were around Reyna's stage.

She's defiant, that much is clear. That's okay. I can make her do what I want.

19

LEO

"Come on, Reyna, we're gonna be late!" I yell down the hallway and walk to the kitchen. My ass is dragging; I'm so tired from working at the club last night. I fill a glass with cold water and down it. At least I'm not hungover. I can't say the same for Saint, and I bet he's dying right now. Haha sucker.

"Calm down, I'm ready," she says, sounding annoyed.

I turn around, once again at a loss for words. She's looking down, adjusting her tits that are squeezed into a tight, black, spaghetti strap dress with a slit coming up high on one leg. Her raven hair falls forward into her face in big waves and her lips are painted in her favorite dark red lipstick.

I quietly clear my throat and my fucking head, and get a grip on myself.

She straightens, and her eyes roam down my body. Without any reaction, she says, "You look good, pet."

I adjust the leather cut on my shoulders, the soft material of my black sweater brushing against my knuckles. I don't know if she's mocking me when she calls me that, but I don't really mind it. If she wanted to dom me, I'd let her.

I don't think a man's masculinity comes in being the dominant one, or any masculinity for that matter. I think it's fun to play on both sides; be dominant and submissive.

———

MY MIND TURNS the entire drive to Orca Bay. Should I ask her or not? Is it an invasion of privacy?

As we pull onto Saint's street and park on the side of the road. I grab her hand as she reaches for the car door handle.

"Have you ever wanted to find your family?" I ask, watching her every move and facial expression for some sign of... anything, really.

Her pink tongue darts out to wet the middle of her lips, and she looks down. "I want to know if I was kidnapped first, then I'd decide if I wanted to find my family. But I don't know how I'd find that out now. The only people who knew about me before I came to the club died a long time ago."

Nodding, I stay quiet and let go of her hand. I'm not going to tell her that we can probably find out, because what if we can't? I don't want to give her a false hope.

We get out of my Mustang—I'm spending the last of the rideable days in my Mustang because Reyna has to carry things with her, like her bag when we go to Second or like today when she's wearing a dress and can't ride on the back of a bike. We're going to have to set aside some time to go for one last ride of the year; I think she secretly enjoyed the last one.

Vans park in the driveway and carry trays of food in through the garage and into the house, so we enter through the front door.

A man greets us and offers to take our coats, but neither of us wears one, so he sends us on our way. I forget Allie's really fucking rich. I mean, we all are, but Allie is new money, classy, actually looks like she's rich, type of rich. The club is secretly rich. We don't really show it unless it's in our homes and cars.

This reception, though? This is all Allie.

White flowers in large marble vases decorate almost every inch of available space, and a huge white rose arch stands in the backyard. A large LED cursive sign says *"We do"* and hangs on the brick wall outside above the dinner table. I mean damn, the party has a dress code—which, to be fair, was just "black" but still.

Mason greets us as we walk into the lush backyard, wearing a white dress shirt with white slacks and his cut.

"You look like a marshmallow." I grin and clap his back as we hug.

But nothing can diminish his shine today. He laughs brightly, smiling wider than I've ever seen. "I can't wait until you fall in love and I get to give you as much shit as you've given me."

"Where's the bar?" I joke, smiling.

Mason chuckles quietly and points to the indoor kitchen where Saint is glaring at the bartender while he makes his drink.

"Do you want something?" I turn to Reyna.

Her black hair swings around as she faces me. "You're asking me?"

I cock my head and smile. Her attitude isn't going to ruin today. My best friend is celebrating his wedding. It's a great day. "I could not."

A ghost of a smile appears on her pouty lips, and I take that as a win. It's very rare that she smiles. "Just a water."

"You don't drink?" I ask, walking toward the bar, and she follows, her head pivoting around as she searches the yard.

"Not really." Her eyes lock on someone across the lawn, and I follow her line of sight. Huntley. Figures, but I like they are growing close. Huntley is friends with the Princess, but Reese is closer to Allie, and I would like Huntley to have her own best friend. I hope Reyna can be that for her. And honestly, Reyna couldn't find a better friend than Huntley. She's a down ass woman and she's honest. She'll tell you when you're being an idiot and then fight anyone else who called you an idiot.

The string quartet on the lawn—I told you this was some rich people shit—stop playing as Allie steps out of the house in a short, bright white dress and boots that literally just look like diamonds spilled down her legs. Mason intertwines his arm with hers and they smile and greet people as they meet Saint in the middle of the patio.

The three of them together—and married—is an odd thought, but it's right. We were all bystanders to the Allie and Saint war, and we all had bets on who she would choose, but seeing them together, it's clear that it's meant to be the three of them.

Reyna wanders off to Huntley's side, and as I look around the backyard, I can't help but notice how many people are missing.

Finn and Huntley stand to the side, Finn surveying the crowd while Huntley stands close to talk to Reyna. Saint, Mason, and Allie talk to a nicely dressed couple. I think the guy is a client of Saint's and the girl has cool black hair but the pieces by her face are blonde. And every once in a while, one of the guys leans down and kisses Allie on the cheek or lips. Cale is standing with Jack by the food table while Reese is talking with a caterer. Other guests mingle around the yard, but we're missing so many brothers today.

Ronan would be over the fucking moon that Saint was married. He'd probably be under that flower arch with a karaoke machine, loudly belting out notes while he downed some rank ass scotch.

Jack and I called Wyatt when we found out Mason and Saint had proposed and begged him to come down for the reception, but he said the club was really busy with the manufacturing of the ghost guns. That he couldn't leave. I'm sure he was telling the truth, but a part of me wonders if he also couldn't come down because of the memories.

We lost a lot this year, and I'm sure it feels like we also gained a lot to the other guys, but it doesn't to me. I'm still alone and fucking anyone who takes my interest. I have my cabin and Second now, but I still think of my lost brothers daily.

It's not like I'm hoping for love or anything. I'm just searching for something to excite me, for some kind of spark.

And Reyna can be exciting sometimes. I guess that's why I'm so interested in her. She's different, and that's exciting.

There's an interruption, Saint clinking a spoon against his glass tumbler, and the crowd quiets down.

"We didn't want any of you assholes at our actual wedding —" Allie elbows Saint in the side and he chuckles but continues, "But we did want you all here for this." Saint reaches into his pocket and pulls out a small ring box. He takes Allie's left hand and holds it. "Al, you loved me when I was at rock bottom, and no matter what I said or did to you, you still loved me. I can never thank you enough for not giving up on me and I'm so deeply sorry that it took me so long to realize that you were always right by my side." Allie wipes at her eyes and Saint clears his throat. "Thank you for saving me, my Queen. You're the only reason I'm still here." He removes Allie's giant ass two diamond ring, and slides on his property ring, putting her engagement ring back on over top.

Saint kisses her and turns her around with his hands on her shoulders. Mason's grin rivals the setting sun in the background.

"I didn't think you could look more beautiful than you did on our wedding day, but you always manage to surprise me." Allie chuckles and Mason takes both of her hands, holding them in his. "You are the most magnetic, intelligent, and resilient woman that I've ever known, and everyday I wonder what I did to catch your eye. I know I don't deserve you, but I will spend everyday trying to be the man that does. You've made me the happiest man in the world, and I can't wait to live our beautiful life. I can't wait to see what the future holds for us because I know we will go through it together." Mason slides his thin black band overtop of Allie's engagement ring, both property bands hugging the two-diamond ring; just like how Allie is always between the two Outlaws.

Allie faces forward, her head swiveling between the two men. "You both have made my heart so full. I couldn't imagine a life without the two of you in it. I know it hasn't always been easy for us, but we made it out the other side together." She grabs their hands. "Thank you for going along with this crazy life and not making me choose. I love you both so much, and I'm so happy to finally be Mrs. Viotto-Underwood."

Everyone in attendance claps and the caterers bring out plates of food and set them on the long wood table.

Reyna and I are seated next to each other, because apparently we go together now, and she excuses herself to go to the restroom after dinner.

I watch the slick fabric hug her swaying hips as she walks away. "Mason didn't invite Miles. I thought they were hacker besties. It would have been a good time to see Reyna and Briar together, too." I add at the end.

Finn crosses his thick arms and leans back in his chair. "He did, but Miles said he couldn't come."

"Really? I wonder why," I think aloud.

Finn smirks and leans closer to me, his voice dropping. "Probably because he doesn't want me telling his new girl about when we tag teamed a girl."

My jaw drops and I close the gap between us; Huntley

doesn't need to hear this, but I want to! "You and Miles? Who?" I ask. I love club gossip!

Finn chuckles and smiles at Huntley, who unknowingly pushes away from the table and leaves to talk to Reese. "It was a girl named Kiki, when I was a different person, long before Huntley. He had just met Cale, and he came to a club party, and Kiki came too. She was going to school at RSU, or just visiting. I can't remember."

I rack my brain trying to remember a Kiki. "I don't think I've ever met her."

Finn shakes his head. "Nah, she hasn't come around in a long time. I think she moved out to the East Coast."

I snicker and pull away from him. "You guys scare her away?"

He shrugs one shoulder, keeping his eyes on Huntley from across the patio. "Maybe. You know how fucking dark he is. He's even worse in bed. Hottest and scariest Eiffel Tower I've ever been a part of."

"Huntley will skin you alive if she knows you're thinking of other girls," I tease.

Finn rolls his eyes lightheartedly. "Huntley is my entire life and universe. There is no one else for me but her, and she's the best fucking lay I've ever had, but it's fun to tease Miles about it."

Finn and I go back and forth for a while longer, talking about our next training session, the strip club, and bikes. And I look around the patio and yard. Reyna hasn't come back from the bathroom, and it's been a minute.

When Mason comes over to talk to us, I excuse myself and wander into the house. Caterers hurry throughout the open living area, taking out the trays of dessert and the dishes from dinner, but no siren in a black dress.

I walk down the hall to the bathroom and as I'm about to knock on the door; it swings open, the burst of air blowing Reyna's dark hair over her shoulders.

She shoves her phone into her small black bag and I look between her and her purse.

"You were gone for a long time. You okay?" I ask skeptical, of what? I'm not sure.

She clears her throat. "The food didn't sit well with me," she snaps. Shoving past me out of the bathroom. "Can we go home? I need to get ready for tonight." She spins around, her hair flying with the motion.

"Yeah." I nod, pulling my keys from my pocket.

I don't know why I'm so pressed to believe the worst about Reyna. Maybe it's because at every turn this year we were shot down or turned on, so it's starting to become second nature to doubt everyone. I hope I learn to let that shit go, because that's not a way to go through life.

20

REYNA

I HOLD MY MOUTH SLACK AS I OUTLINE MY LIPS WITH THE MAROON lip pencil.

A cloud of sickly sweet perfume wafts over me, seeping into my nose and open mouth. I want to puke. "I caught your dance last night. It was so good; do you take classes?" One of the other dancers cocks her head and blinks at me.

"No," I answer flatly, closing my mouth so I don't eat any more of her saccharine scent.

"Oh." Her face falls, and she turns forward, rifling through her makeup bag.

A new feeling washes over me. Guilt for cutting her off so quickly. I could recommend she talk to Huntley. She said she went to a pole studio sometimes, but I don't want her to talk to Huntley. Huntley is my... friend, I suppose. Since when have I become possessive over a person?

I push the foreign feeling aside and finish applying my makeup. I don't have time for friendships, and I've truthfully only ever had one friendship with Hector, and he and I weren't even really friends, more like close boss and employee.

I shouldn't even be thinking of such trivial things. I'm the opening dancer again tonight, so I need to get mentally ready.

I decide to wear some color tonight: a blood red lace, matching set and zip up my black knee-high boots.

Leo steps into the locker room, every pair of eyes in the room turning to him and admiring him. And I can definitely see why. I've known since he knelt by my bedside at La Lujuria. He's attractive, and it's not even just the way he looks.

It's the way he carries himself, with a lightness like the world doesn't get him down. And an aura that walks the line of confidence and arrogance: not too much that you want to reject him just to knock him down a peg, but enough that it's actually charming.

His easy eyes fall on me and I know he's here to escort me to the stage.

I like we get escorted to and from the stage. We were expecting the first weekend to be packed, and for the following nights to be less busy. We can roam around the club while we're not dancing. Talk to customers, offer private dances, or get drinks for ourselves; but when we're going on for a dance, we get walked to the stage.

The slow, sultry beats of "One of the Girls" by The Weeknd fills the club.

"Are you going to be a good girl and not dance on anyone?" Leo huskily asks, leaning closer to me, his dark eyes facing forward.

I smirk. "I don't enjoy being a good girl." I brush past him and take the steps up to the stage.

Strutting to the pole, I eye the crowd, and notice something odd and equally infuriating: all the chairs are gone from around my stage. Everyone has to stand.

This mother fucker. He took all the chairs so I couldn't give lap dances. Smart.

I can't react though, so I take hold of the pole and rise off of my feet, starting a slow spin around the pole. I tuck my legs and climb the pole, positioning my body over one of my hands so I can lean against it while I invert and straddle my legs, my free hair falling down like a thick, black curtain.

Twisting my body around, I settle the pole between my ass and let go of the pole with one hand first, then slowly the second hand, letting my legs hold me upright as I slowly turn around the pole.

I grab the pole and twist my body again, so my back is toward the floor and grab one of my ankles, extending the opposite one in the splits.

I let my back softly land on the floor, and roll over, staying in my splits. Putting my hands on the floor, I pivot my body so I'm in middle splits and slightly lift up, popping my ass to the beat and then laying my chest and face down on the stage. Reaching behind me, I unclasp my bra, and sit up, pulling the straps down my arms and looking around the crowd. I had choreographed a lap dance into this routine so I need to figure out how to fill that space.

And would you look at that... in the middle of the standing crowd is Leo, sitting in a chair and staring at me. The only chair in front of my stage happens to be filled by him. No coincidence there. Very well.

I drop my bra to the stage and lay down, lifting my legs over my body and rolling over. I land on my knees and spin around, tossing my hair as I go. Crawling across the stage, I make eye contact with other customers as I work my way by, dropping my body to the floor every few steps.

I'm half a stage away from him. I roll to the side, throwing my legs apart, and I turn and land on my stomach in a pile of bills. Pushing my ass toward the edge of the stage, and giving everyone a great view of my bare ass in my thong, I push onto my knees and spin so I'm facing the front, then crawl another two steps until I'm right in front of Leo.

I slide off of the side of the stage and onto my toes. The people gathered around my stage watch as I walk to Leo, and he raises his chin as I get near.

I lightly rest my hand on his shoulder and straddle him, putting the other hand on his knee and squeezing hard.

Leaning back, I gyrate my hips like I'm riding him, and for a brief, weak second, his eyes dart down to where he wishes we're joined.

Smirking, I lean forward, putting my naked breast in his face and whisper into his ear. "Nobody makes me do anything that I don't want to do." Swinging my leg around, I climb off of his lap and walk back to the locker room before the song has ended.

21

LEO

S UNLIGHT BEAMS THROUGH THE FLOOR-TO-CEILING WINDOWS AND into my loft bedroom, waking me up. Groaning, I roll over and check the time on my phone. Noon.

Being nocturnal was more fun when I was staying up late, drinking and partying, not running a full strip club, and taking care of customers and strippers all night. Although last night had been a little more play than work.

Reyna tried to hide it, but I saw the surprise and spitefulness in her eyes when she saw I got rid of the chairs for her dance. I was serious that I didn't want her dancing on anyone, but I know that's so wrong. She's a stripper, just like the rest, so she should be treated like the others. Not given special treatment or having things and opportunities to make money taken away from her just because I'm jealous.

Which, by the way, that took a long fucking time to come to terms with. I've never been jealous in my life, and then to feel it so intensely for one woman. Wild.

Grabbing my phone from the nightstand, I unlock it to find a message from Mason.

MASON:

Did you get what I asked for?

He's asking if I've gotten any DNA from Reyna yet.

LEO:

No, I'm working on it.

Sighing, I run my hand down my face. It's been a day. How does he expect me to get something like that so quickly?

MASON:

I don't have anywhere to start until you get it.

LEO:

I know. I'll get it soon.

I know he's just trying to do what I asked him, but I really don't know what to do. Should I keep a straw she drank out of? I could probably get that from the club, but there's a high chance it would get mixed up with someone else's drink or thrown away before I could get to it. Maybe I could save a cup she drinks out of here at the house. Surely she wouldn't notice a glass gone missing, right?

Maybe I should just be vigilant and watch for an opportunity instead of planning it out. That's more my style, anyway.

Cabinets open and close in the kitchen downstairs and I roll out of bed; Reyna is awake.

I grab a black pair of sweatpants from the basket on my floor that I have yet to put away, and slide them up my legs before heading for the wood stairs and taking them down.

Reyna's in the corner of the kitchen, pouring a mug of coffee from the basic coffee machine that I stole from the clubhouse when I moved out.

Pieces of her tattoo peek through the small black top she's

wearing. It takes up the entirety of her back. The thin black lines swirling into the scales of a snake that climbs up her back, from her waist to her opposite shoulder. The serpent twines around intricate flowers, similar to the ones that fall down her arm. Some may think that tattoos are manly or trashy, but they're wrong. Tattoos are art, and Reyna's makes her look more delicate.

But she's not delicate. This woman is sharp and cunning.

And that makes her even more interesting to me.

Crossing my arms, I prop my hip against the peninsula counter and watch her. She spoons sugar into the mug and then turns, and walks to the fridge at the end of the cabinets.

"You watch me so often that I should start charging you," she says, not even turning to look at me once.

"I like watching you," I admit. And it's true. The way she walks, dances, talks. She makes everything look so beautiful.

She turns around, finally facing me, and I notice she's not wearing any makeup. She's still just as beautiful.

Reyna raises the white mug to her pink lips, her light blue eyes look wider without her thick lashes on. Then they close and her nose scrunches up.

I laugh uncontrollably. She's never shown so much expression on her beautiful face. "This is disgusting." She tips the mug over and dumps the brown liquid down the drain.

Chest still bouncing from laughter, I say, "I'll take you out for coffee if you'll help me with yard work today."

Her shoulders fall sharply as she exhales, but her face doesn't betray a single emotion. "Fine. What are we doing?"

"I have to replace a board that's rotted out on the dock, and I want to do it before the rainy season starts."

"Fine," she says.

I tilt my head toward her bedroom, eyeing her black leggings and black crop top bra thing. "Go put a jacket on. We'll take the bike." I wait and watch her face carefully. Happiness rises inside of me when a small smile pulls at the corner of her lips before she ducks her head to turn and put the mug in the sink. But before I can make any more of an ass of myself, I turn around and head upstairs to grab a hoodie and my cut. I can't care about her happiness. There are too many unanswered questions right now.

Bouncing down the stairs, I shove my wallet and phone in the inside pocket of my cut. My eyes fall on Reyna with her back to me, looking out over the front of my property. And I can't lie. Seeing her in lace or topless is really fucking hot, but seeing her in leather is something else entirely. Her fitted, black leather jacket hugs her tight waist as she stands with her hands in her pockets.

Her head turns, her long, black ponytail slicing through the air. "Took you long enough," she quips before pushing the door open and walking outside. Chuckling silently, I follow her.

Reyna watches me swing my leg over my bike and sit down, hefting the thing upright before I offer her my hand.

She ignores me, placing her hand on my shoulder and getting on like a pro. She's always confident, I'll give her that. The only thing that betrays her stern self is the death grip she has around my stomach, but that can be one of our secrets.

Her musky cherry scent creeps up my nostrils as I start the engine and my bike roars to life. I could get high off of this scent.

I pat her hands before I grab the handlebars and gun it down the dirt road.

She doesn't scream this time.

I slow the bike to a stop in front of a small coffee shop, and Reyna's hands slowly unlock and retreat from my stomach.

"I don't know why you're in such a hurry to die," she snaps, climbing off my bike.

"There's no sense in living if you don't feel alive."

She eyes the shop. "Hmm," she hums. "I expected you to bring me to a bikini barista." She turns and slides her eyes down my body as I stand from the bike. "You seem like the womanizing type."

I bite my lip to stifle my laugh. "First, you're judgmental, bikini baristas have great coffee. Second, I am."

Her shoulders shake once, and I mentally pat myself on the back. "Was that a laugh?" I ask mockingly. "Wow, careful, next you might actually start enjoying my company."

Reyna rolls her eyes, but I don't miss the ghost of a smile on her full lips. "Don't flatter yourself."

We order our drinks inside, and after I pay, we head outside with our coffees to enjoy the last remnants of the warm weather.

Reyna's black sunglasses cover most of her face as she glances around the busy street and walkway.

"You don't talk... ever," I finally break the silence.

She sets the cardboard cup on the table. "I talk sometimes."

"You flirt, insult, or give flirty insults," I laugh.

Her head turns to look at me, my reflection staring back at me in her sunglasses. "Where is the need to say more?" she asks calmly.

I shrug one shoulder. I'll make friends with anyone who comes along, so it's always hard for me when people aren't immediately open. Strangely, those are always the ones that I form the closest friendships with: Jack and Huntley.

"I don't know. I mean, we live together, so it'd be nice to have a conversation with you sometime," I push.

"What do you want to talk about, Leo?" she snaps, her pink tongue darting out to wet her lips.

"What do you want to do in the future? Stripping isn't really a lifelong career."

Reyna sighs before standing. "If you want my help with your

dock, we need to go. I'm meeting Huntley later to practice our routine for next weekend."

I nod and push away from the table. "Okay." I watch her walk to the trash can by the door. Her cup would be a good DNA source, but she would notice me keeping it. I don't think I could snag the lid without her knowing either.

She tosses the empty cup in the can and I throw mine in after her, staring at the piece of trash at the bottom of the bag.

———

WE DITCHED our leather before coming down to the dock. Reyna sits on one side of the gaping hole where I tore out two boards, and I'm kneeling on the other side.

It's silent. The sounds of rustling leaves and me asking for tools fill the gap between us, but it's comfortable. Being with Jack for the last year has taught me that silence isn't awkward. Actually, to be able to sit in silence with someone and still be connected to them is one of the best things.

I grunt and bang the nail into the wood as sweat drips down my forehead and my knuckles ache. I can do this type of labor, but that doesn't mean I enjoy it.

To be honest, I liked working at Finn's body shop because I got to be with Jack and Finn, but that shit was for the birds.

I was always covered in grease or paint, and I really don't like being told what to do all the time. Graduating from prospect to patched member was one of the best days of my life, partly because of that.

I pick my head up and glance at Reyna when I notice that she's not taking the tools I'm trying to hand her. I caught her glancing at the small rowboat that's tied up to the side of the dock earlier, and she's staring at it again.

"Do you want to go out on it?" I ask, tossing the hammer into my tool bag and collecting up the nails I didn't use. She blinks at me, and I laugh, catching her drift. "I'll row."

Her lips scrunch up under her nose. "Will it hold the both of us?"

"Only one way to find out, Siren." I grin, pushing off of the dock and stepping onto the small wooden boat. This thing came with the house and I've never used it. We really might sink in the pond, but that's alright, it's not a big pond.

Reyna takes my outstretched hand as she slides into the small boat from the dock and settles down across from me.

Our knees touch as I set the oars in place and push us away from the dock.

"Are there any fish?" Reyna asks, looking down into the blue water.

I shake my head, rowing us toward the middle of the pond. "No. I thought about it but haven't decided yet."

We arrive in the middle and I pull in the oars, letting us idle as the ripples around the boat slowly dissipate. The sun shines down on us, almost reflecting off of Reyna's dark, shiny hair.

She closes her eyes and raises her face toward the sky. A content and peaceful look softening her face.

"I didn't go outside a lot while on the island. Not unless I was going to Seattle for something," she says, her eyes still closed as she soaks in the sunlight.

"Why?" I ask softly. I don't want to scare her into shutting up. I want her to keep going. I need to know more, for my sake and the clubs.

"There wasn't anything to do, so I slept during the day and at night I was working." Finally, she lowers her face and opens her eyes, right at me. "I never thought of a future when I was at the club. Everything was too unclear, and I knew that my life wasn't my own. I belonged to the club, so they would decide my future."

"And what about now?" I ask. I'm hanging onto every word she says, like she's my favorite novel.

She looks over the water and the trees surrounding the pond. "I want to make enough money to get me the hell out of Washington and live a quiet and uneventful life in a penthouse in New York, or Seoul, or Paris. Somewhere where no one will pay attention to me."

I wish I could say I didn't know why her answer knocked me in the gut like a sucker punch, but I do, and neither realization makes me feel any better.

22

REYNA

"Okay, so then what if I do this?" Huntley wraps one leg around the pole and straightens herself out, her long body extending from the pole sideways. "And then you come back upright and slowly lower yourself on top of me."

I watch her talk, hanging upside down on the pole as we spin slowly. I do as she says, pushing myself back upright and wrapping my thighs around the pole and carefully sliding down the pole until I'm hovering above her pelvis.

"You're dirty." I smirk, tossing my head back and using my arms to pump myself up and down.

Huntley laughs, her head falling backward and her waist-length, white hair gliding against the wood floor in her ponytail. "I have to live up to your reputation."

Huntley loosens her grip and slides to the floor, her back settling gently on the hardwood.

I use the soft towel to dab at the sweat on my forehead and neck while Huntley lies on the floor with her eyes closed, her chest slowing with every deep breath.

We mapped out our entire routine and ran through it a few

times to make sure it flowed perfectly, and I'm impressed. It's going to be really hot.

"How's Leo's cabin?" Huntley asks, lifting her torso from the floor, her exposed stomach flexing.

"Fine," I answer evenly, lowering myself to sit on the floor in front of her. What is she getting at?

"And how's Leo?" She cocks her head.

I watch her from under my lashes. "I'm sure he's just fine."

She leans back, her long fingers unscrewing the cap off of her water bottle. "I'm sure he is, now that you're living with him."

Smirking, I roll my eyes. "He would be better than fine if I were fucking him."

Her playful grin turns serious. "Just be careful, okay? Don't hurt him, but also, watch out for him, too."

"Are you warning me or threatening me?" I laugh.

Huntley cringes, her nose scrunching up and her brows pulling together. "Both," she chuckles. "He's my best friend, but I also really like you, so I don't want either of you to get hurt."

"Good to know." I turn away and reach for my bag, pulling it toward me by the long strap.

"'Good to know,' that's it?" Huntley screeches, her voice rising and her mouth hanging open.

"What do you want me to say?" I hold in my laughter, but still smile, so she knows I'm playing along with her fake outrage. At least, I'm pretty sure it's fake.

And it's confirmed when she relaxes and her mouth slants to one side. "You don't have to be alone anymore, Reyna. You can lean on the club now."

Shaking my head lightly, I lick my lips. "I don't know how to lean on anyone," I admit.

Huntley reaches for my hand and clasps my fingers that are running over the smooth leather strap of my duffle. "Anytime that you're feeling something, you can share it with me. Whenever something happens, you can come to me and I'll help you, no matter what it is."

"Why would you do that?" I ask too quickly, hanging onto her every word.

Huntley squeezes my hand softly. The sun pours in through the window and shines off of her prominent cheekbones. Her lips curve into a smile. "Because it's what friends do."

I have to look away from Huntley, and I stare at our hands instead. It feels nice to have someone want to be there for me, when I've been alone for my entire life. I don't know anything different, but I'd like to.

Ding! The bell over the front door chimes and my head whips around, my heart stopping in my chest.

"We're closed today." Huntley pushes off of the floor, her mile long legs making her look endlessly tall from where I sit on the floor.

His dirty blonde hair hangs in his eyes as they run over the small studio slowly. "Oh, I'm sorry. I saw the car out front and since the door was unlocked, I thought you were open." Huntley crosses her arms across her chest as she watches him and I try to catch my breath, my eyes wide in surprise. "I was looking for information on your classes." His thin lips slide into a smile that, to anyone else, would look innocent, but I know him.

"This is a women only studio, and as I said before, we're *closed,*" Huntley draws out the last word.

He nods, his lips staying in that creepy smile. "My apologies. Good afternoon, ladies." He backs toward the door slowly, and he finally looks down at me on the floor. As if in slow motion, his smile slides into a wide smirk and he winks at me before he turns and pushes through the studio door.

"Ew." Huntley scrunches her nose as she walks to the door and flips the lock.

My heart seems to make up for the time that it stopped and now beats a mile a minute, and I stay quiet.

On cue, my phone vibrates against the wood floor in my duffle, and I snatch it out, not being able to wait to read what his text will say. Because there's no way he wouldn't walk in here and *not* say something to me afterward.

UNKNOWN:

That was your warning. Hurry up, little whore.

Huntley stays at the door, watching as his car pulls out of the parking lot. "You ready to go?" She looks away from the window and at me, and my stomach turns with unease.

I feel regret for the first time in my life, and it feels really awful.

23

REYNA

THE MILLIONTH BANG SINCE I WOKE UP CAUSES ME TO ROLL MY eyes from where I lay on the couch. Leo has been working in his bathroom all day and I've had the pleasure of having a front row-seat to him swearing and banging things around upstairs. Occasionally he'll stomp down the stairs and yank open the refrigerator, refill his stainless steel cup and stare out of the front window while he angrily gulps down water, before stomping back up the stairs and tossing more stuff around.

So overall, I think the renovation is going great.

His shoes thump on the wooden stairs once again, but this time he turns down the hallway toward our shared bathroom.

"I'll make dinner after I shower. I just need to get this shit off of me first!" he calls over his shoulder and goes into the bathroom.

The shower turns on, and I rest my head back on the couch pillow. Finally, some peace.

We both woke up around noon, and Leo was nice enough to start his project until after I had gotten up.

I found him sitting on the porch in a rocking chair while he drank from a coffee mug. I haven't touched that shit since the first time I tried to drink his rancid coffee, but no worries. I ordered an espresso machine and some higher quality coffee. I had to get it on rush shipping, so it'll be here this week.

But cheap coffee aside, I did secretly stand inside and watch him for a few moments. His far off stare as he rocked back and forth, occasionally bringing the white mug to his arched lips and taking a drink. His brown hair was messy and pieces fell onto his forehead and brushed against his thick brows. Eventually, I had to pull myself away and take myself to the kitchen for some eggs and juice.

I couldn't continue to stare at him, wondering what it would have been like to be born into a normal family, and find Leo by some stroke of luck. We hit it off and date for a while before he proposes to me at the tailgate before one of the University football games or at Christmas in front of our families. We buy this cabin because we love the bones of the house and the property and Leo spends late nights and early mornings turning it into my dream home. I wake up in the mornings and watch him on the porch, thinking how wonderful my life is.

Where the hell do I get off imagining such ludicrous things?

I want to slap myself for being so unrealistic in a time where I cannot afford to fuck up. Messing this up means losing my only shot of having something real.

But I feel my heart softening for Huntley and Leo; in a way that it never has for anyone else.

I fear that's going to end badly.

The door at the end of the hall swings open and Leo struts out, once again in nothing but a towel wrapped around his trim waist. He keeps his eyes on me as he walks down the short hallway, but it feels like he walks an entire runway while my eyes fall down his muscled body; a skull with snakes surrounding it inked onto his chest. The same design that he wears on the back of his club cut.

With a smirk, he turns and starts up the stairs. Pulling the towel off his hips, he walks up the stairs completely naked.

My breath catches in my throat as I watch his thick, muscled thighs and tight ass disappear up the stairs. Unfortunately for me, from where I'm laying, I'm not able to see the front of him, but the back sure doesn't disappoint.

He comes down a few minutes later in sweats and a big tee shirt, and goes straight to the kitchen.

Eyeing him, I get up and follow.

"Seems you should be the one on the pole, since you love taking your clothes off so much." I stop on the opposite side of the peninsula counter and lean against it, watching Leo root around in the refrigerator.

He chuckles, his head still in the fridge. "I thought I'd try to make you more comfortable since I see you topless at work." He brings raw hamburgers to the counter and opens the package.

"I can give you some lessons if you want, or Huntley can; she's pretty good." I watch as Leo places the meat on a large plate and shuffles through his seasonings.

"Is she? I didn't know." He sounds distracted as he unscrews lids and season the burgers.

"She's great. She should be working at Second."

Leo scoffs and puts the small bottles away. "We wouldn't have any guests because Finn would assault anyone that went to Huntley's stage."

"She's dancing with me this weekend at the Halloween party," I argue.

Leo glances at me as he walks past me, leaving the meat on the counter. "Yeah, and I'm still shocked that Huntley ever agreed, and that Finn hasn't blown up the club yet, so she can't."

Turning around, I rest my lower back against the counter as Leo opens the front door and goes to the grill.

The sun started setting a while ago, and now it's just peeking out over the tops of the trees on the other side of the pond. The orange rays and pink sky reflect off of the water and bathe the evening in a warm and inviting hue.

Leo closes the lid on the grill and turns to come back inside. He opens the door, freezing just as he's about to step inside. He turns around and I watch intently. What's going on?

A woman walks around the side of the house. Long brunette hair hanging over her shoulders and a big smile plastered on her face. Leo looks back at me, purses his lips and then turns around to look at the woman again.

"Hey, Mom," he calls, leaving the door open as he hurries off the porch to take the giant boxes she's carrying.

Oh, my god... his mom. Kill me now.

She hands the boxes over and then follows behind him as he comes into the cabin.

"I opened them after they were delivered and figured you needed them, so I brought them over," Leo's mom says cheer-fully, her smile just as warm as her sons.

"Thank you. I didn't mean to have them sent to your house," he replies, setting the boxes down by the stairs.

"Oh! Hello!" Leo's mom's eyes widen as they fall on me. "I'm sorry. I should have called before coming over." She turns to Leo. "I didn't mean to interrupt your date."

Leo straightens up at the same time that my spine snaps upright. "This isn't a date, Mom. Reyna works for the club and I offered her my spare room while she gets settled into Merrill Hill." *Only a slight lie, but sure.*

Leo's mom walks toward me, her hand extended. "I'm Lucia, Leo's mom."

Taking her hand, I smile. "I'm Reyna. I work at the Second Circle."

Her hazel eyes widen again; the color so similar to Leo's. "Oh, the strip club?" I nod, humming and gauging her reaction.

How would she react to learning her son lives with a stripper and runs the strip club? "I've taken a couple of classes at the pole studio in town; it's so much fun! No wonder you're in great shape!"

That was pleasant. "Ma," Leo groans. "Why are you going to pole classes?"

Lucia smirks at Leo's back as he walks past us and into the kitchen. "To spice things up, Son." *God, Leo looks just like her!*

"Ma, I take care of you so you don't have to date deadbeats and try to spice things up." I can hear the veiled panic in Leo's voice, and it's sweet that he worries over his mother, and that he takes care of her since it seems his dad isn't in the picture.

"What if he's not a deadbeat?" Lucia counters, the smile never leaving her face.

"Are you dating?" Leo snaps, turning around to stare at his mother.

She shrugs. "I started seeing someone."

Leo turns back around, shaking his head. "I have to meet him." He yanks open the refrigerator and Lucia playfully winks at me.

Leo pulls out lettuce, onions, and tomatoes and takes them to the sink.

"Well, I was just dropping those tiles off. I'll let you two get back to your dinner," Lucia says.

"Stay for dinner, Ma." Leo looks over his shoulder at us.

"Are you sure?" She looks between us.

I nod and shrug, but Leo speaks up. "Yes. That way, I know you're not with him."

Lucia laughs and sets her purse down on the counter before walking into the kitchen and kissing her son on the cheek. She steps beside him and takes the tomato from him. "My sweet boy, I'm the one who is supposed to protect you." She turns on the tap and washes the fruit.

Leo stays by her side and watches over her, standing at least a foot above her. "You protected me for eighteen years. Now it's my turn."

She turns to look at Leo, and I can see her hazel eyes sparkling. "No, baby. My turn is never over. I'll watch over you long after I've left this earth."

Leo places a quick kiss on the top of Lucia's head. "Don't talk about that, Ma." She smiles up at him and pats his arm before reaching for a knife from the wooden block on the counter.

Leo takes the plate of meat outside, leaving Lucia and me alone in the kitchen.

She carries the washed fruit on a cutting board and the knife over to the counter where I am and places them down.

She cuts into the onion. "His father left before he was born, never came back. He's been very protective of me since he started to understand that."

"I'm sorry," I offer, not really sure what else to say. I didn't know we were going to share our hardships over the cutting board.

She shrugs one shoulder, continuing to chop. "Leo kept me busy enough; I wouldn't have had the time to date even if I tried."

I nod. "You raised a good man," I say. And she did. Leo let me into his cabin when he didn't have to. I know they wanted to get me out of the clubhouse, but he didn't have to take me into his home.

Lucia smiles proudly, grabbing the tomato and slicing into it. "Thank you. I know he's still young, but I'm proud of the responsibility he's taken on in the club and the men he's surrounded himself with. I think they are a good influence on him."

Young? Wait, how old *is* Leo? "I guess I never realized, how old is Leo?" I ask.

She chuckles, "Twenty-two."

He's younger than me. Now his bright charm makes sense, but he's only four years younger than me.

The door swings open and Leo steps inside with the large plate, now with cooked burgers on it instead of raw ones. "Are you talking about how great I am?" Leo asks brightly.

"Aye," Lucia groans. "Quit being big-headed," she chides.

Leo laughs and sets the serving plate down on the peninsula. I watch him as he grabs three plates from the cabinet by the sink and the hamburger buns off of the counter. I watch him with different eyes than I had previously. Leo is like a dahlia. He has layers upon layers of petals, and just when I think I've reached the last one, he exposes another.

24

LEO

My bike rumbles beneath me as I pull it to a stop beside my brothers. It was damn chilly tonight, almost too cold to ride it, but I'm going to stick it out until I can't any longer, and then put the thing away in Finn's home shop for the winter. I really should build a garage out at the cabin, but I'll finish the cabin before I start on anything else.

Everyone else has the same mindset as me, because I park at the end of a line of five bikes.

Light spills from the windows on the side of the clubhouse and the tall lights in the parking lot. Finn sits on the table of a picnic table, his black boots resting on the seat, with a lit joint to his lips.

"Hey." I incline my head as I reach him.

He takes a long drag and then ashes the joint out in a large glass ashtray. "Hey." He smiles. We all smile again, and it's really nice to see.

We walk into the clubhouse together, a few club girls walk around, sitting at the bar and laughing over drinks. Everyone is happier without death breathing down our backs and taking out our brothers.

I was naive when I joined the club. Young and hot headed. I knew the club was in a war years prior, but I never imagined it would go down again. I never imagined I would experience so much loss in such a short amount of time. It changed us all a little bit, some more than others.

I want to believe that I wouldn't have died if it had come down to it. Maybe I'm being naive and arrogant again, but mostly it's determination and fear. If I had died, my mom would have found some way to curse me in the afterlife for putting myself in danger. If she knew what really happened in the club, she would drag me out here and never let me out of the house again.

"Did you walk here?" Cale snarks as Finn and I step into the chapel, closing the doors behind us.

"Ha ha." I mock boredly. "I live the furthest. Sorry you fuckers have to wait a few more minutes."

"It doesn't help that you also ride the slowest." Finn grins as we pull our seats out beside each other.

Rolling my eyes, I take my seat. "Now you know that's a damn lie."

"Yeah, yeah. Can we get on with it?" Saint interrupts, quieting us all. "We have business to discuss."

"Alright, alright," Finn chuckles. "Go on then, Prezzy."

Saint shoots daggers at Finn. "Why haven't I kicked you out yet?"

Finn barks out a laugh, his head falling backward. "Because then I'd kick your ass and you know you wouldn't win."

Saint rolls his eyes, rolling his seat closer to the table. "I'm sure a bullet would slow your big ass down, though." Saint huffs out a breath. "Anyway, the California chapter reached out. Their ghost guns are ready and they want our bullets. They want to team up, sort of make the Outlaws a one stop shop: bullets and guns."

"It would be a safer transaction," Cale agrees. "Trading with guys we trust, we know they won't betray or stiff us."

"That's exactly what I was thinking." Saint smiles, but then it slowly fades. "Look, I know there's always going to be some type of danger in this life, but I promise to do everything I can to send you home to your Old Ladies at the end of the day." His gaze falters to the table. "And I'm sorry for the call I made. I'm sorry for the war I started." His ice blue eyes raise, and they land on each of us, one by one. "I'll never risk a single one of you again."

"None of what happened was your fault, Saint," Cale says.

Saint turns his stony gaze to Callum. "It was my call."

"One any one of us would have made," Finn interjects. "We fight and die for the Outlaws, just like we live and fuck for them, too. We all knew what we were signing up for when we patched in."

"Stop blaming yourself, brother," I add, and Saint nods. I wish we could take the grief and regret off of his shoulders. I know it weighs down on him as heavy as the world.

"I have a new prospect," Saint continues. I guarantee everyone's assholes clench at those four words. "I know." He holds up one hand, nodding. "But we are dangerously low on members, so we have to let others in." He looks at Mason. "I want to know every fucking detail of this kid before he ever even lays eyes on this compound. I want to know where he went to school, every-where he's worked, when he took his first shit, and how many breaths he takes a day. If you can't find concrete evidence that he's *not* a fucking fed, he's not coming in. He'll have an extra long hang around time so we can fully vet him before giving him a cut."

Mase nods. "Got it, Prez. Give me his name after this and I'll start running him."

"Alright." Saint bangs the gavel against the table. "Get the fuck out of here and go home."

Slowly, we all stand and leave the chapel, but none of us reach the front door. We all stop by the bar and take a seat. A club girl pours drinks for us and brings out bowls of chips and nuts and shit.

I smile, wrapping my arm around an ever silent Jack. It's been a while since we all sat here as a club and just enjoyed each other's company. Looks like Huntley might have to come pick me and Finn up tonight.

25

REYNA

Groaning and soft footsteps on the stairs pull my attention from the TV. Leo's sweatpants are slung low on his hips, that delicious v popping out and tempting me. His arms flex as he raises them to rub viciously at his eyes.

"You look like shit," I bite at him, turning away to focus on the show on the screen again.

"You sound like a bitch," he counters, but there's no venom behind it.

Leo walks straight to the kitchen, opening up the cabinet and using my new espresso machine: what a dick. He's silent while he brews his coffee, the tv drowning out the light hum of the machine.

He lands deftly in the leather chair beside the couch and sips from the mug. His dark hair is strewn about and his eyes are closed as he rests his head against the back of the seat.

"You were out late last night." I was woken up as he stumbled inside, and I peeked out of my bedroom door and watched him clumsily make his way upstairs. After closing my door, I heard him come downstairs to the bathroom and then back upstairs, and everything was silent for the rest of the night.

He takes another sip, keeping his eyes closed as he opens his mouth to speak. "I had church." I don't say anything else, just glare at him; anger settling in my stomach. He cracks one eye open and watches me. "Are you jealous?" His grin grows, and he opens the other eye, sitting up to lean closer to me.

"What would I be jealous of?" I snap, glaring at him even harder.

His tongue runs across his lip and I can't help it. I follow it. "I left you here, was gone for hours doing who knows what, then I came home drunk off my ass and didn't look for you."

My teeth sink into my cheek to hold back all the hatred I want to spew at him, because he's right, and anything I say right now will only confirm that to him. He can't win. He can't know.

I did stay up wondering when he was going to come back, what he was doing, and after waiting for hours, I finally fell asleep. Only to be woken up to him coming home drunk. I've never experienced something like this.

"What if I told you I did look for you?" he asks, looking into my eyes, his hazel ones red and bloodshot, but still clear. "I stood outside your door and contemplated coming inside, but I made myself go to sleep."

"Why?" I whisper.

"Because I don't want to fuck you when I'm fucked up." We stare at each other for a long time, so many feelings pass between us: lust, longing, jealousy, excitement, nervousness. But then he leans back in his seat and closes his eyes, taking another sip of coffee. "Pack a bag for a few days. You're staying with Huntley."

Every emotion in me halts, like I was just splashed with ice water. "What?"

"The club has to go down to California, so you're staying with Huntley." My mouth hangs open, and Leo continues.

"Don't sass me. Do you really want to stay out here with no car? No one delivers this far out, so you'll be stranded."

I push off the couch and try to keep my footsteps even as I walk to the kitchen to put my coffee mug in the dishwasher. I'm disappointed and mad. I wish he had asked me to go with him instead of staying behind. And what's worse? I'm not sure which part of me is more upset. The part that secretly is starting to like Leo or the part that needs to like him.

I pack a bag with a few changes of clothes. I'm not really sure what we'll do, so I pack a little of everything to be prepared.

As I'm leaving the bathroom with my toiletries, Leo is coming down the hall. I brush past him to head into my room, but he grabs my arm to halt me.

With my back against the doorframe, I look up into his hazel eyes. Pieces of his brown hair hang in his eyes and his bare chest burns into my shirt as he steps in close to me. "I don't know why I'm promising this shit to you, because this isn't me, but I might as well since I know I'll mean it." he pauses, his eyes darting between mine as he looks down at me, my arm pressed between us as he keeps ahold of it. "I promise I won't even look at another woman while I'm on this trip. I won't do anything for you to be jealous over. You don't have to worry while I'm away."

"Take me with you," I whisper.

Leo smirks and shakes his head. "Sorry, Siren." He lets go of my arm and steps away from me. "Your song won't work on me this time." He steps into the bathroom and I hear the cabinet door open. I hurry into my room and toss my toiletry bag into my bag.

I'm fucked. I'm so fucked, and not in any way I've ever been before.

26

LEO

"Fuck, that was a long drive," I groan, stretching my back as I climb out of the driver's seat of the club van.

Lights shine out of the windows of a simple, paneled house with tall palm trees standing on the sides. It's just past midnight, so the street lights illuminate the cement sidewalk and the ocean waves crashing against the sand fill the air.

It's damn nice, and we've only been here less than a minute.

"At least you had a heater when we were in Washington," Mase whines.

I roll my eyes. He's such a baby. "You could have been in the van, but you wanted to ride your bike."

The paint chipped door opens, and a big ugly fucker walks out, his boots thumping on the wooden porch.

Wyatt's wavy brown hair is down to his shoulders, with caramel streaks running through the stands. His thick beard is cleaned up, and his bulging arms cross over his chest.

"It's about fucking time!" he shouts, his mouth opening into a giant grin.

I swear the porch shakes under his steps as he descends the three stairs to the sidewalk. He grabs Saint in an unexpected hug and claps his back hard with his giant palm. He makes his way through everybody. I'm pretty sure he and Finn were in a competition for who could slap the hardest, and I know they're going to have bruises on their backs because of it.

"Playboy," he smiles, opening his arms in front of me.

"MC Jesus," I reply, stepping into his embrace. Wyatt is a good friend, and although he's quiet and he stays to himself a lot, he was always there to listen. And call me a shit head for all of my antics.

Jack laughs under his breath, but Wyatt barks a loud laugh. I realize that I've missed him. We came into the club at the same time. We're brothers. Just because he switched chapters doesn't mean that's changed.

"Park the van in the garage, then come inside and have a drink. We'll get our prospects to unload it." Wyatt moves to clap a hand on Jack's shoulder, remembering he's not the biggest fan of affection.

Jack and I drive the van into the detached garage at the end of the driveway and park it, leaving it for the California prospects to unload.

I take out my phone; the light shining in my face.

LEO:

Do you miss me, Siren?

I don't expect her to respond, so I pocket my phone and follow Jack into the house through the back door. The house is already loud with the raucous of loud talking and laughter. The kitchen is packed, Saint and Mason sit at the shitty, round table with a few of the California brothers and Wyatt. Someone's bent over, reaching into the fridge, and when he stands back up and sees us, he steps aside to let us take a drink out.

I hand Jack a beer, and put my hand on his shoulder, stepping in close to speak in his ear. "We'll find a quiet corner to hang out," I promise.

Jack trails behind me as I walk into the living room. Finn and Cale are playing darts with a California brother while others sit around and drink and talk. A few girls walk around, of course, but I don't even give them a second thought—which is not normal for me, but they're not...

REYNA:

Do you miss me, Playboy?

I haven't had one thought of another woman since I freed this one from a bed in a blood-soaked sex club; black makeup running down her face, and her beautiful body exposed for anyone to see. I don't know what horrors she witnessed before me, but I swore right then, when our eyes met, that she would never see any more. I'll never fucking tell her that, though.

LEO:

How'd you find out about that?

REYNA:

People talk.

Goddamn Huntley. But I'm glad they're friends.

Jack and I take seats on the beat up couch, and I eye the baggies laying on the coffee table in front of us.

"What's ours is yours, brothers. Help yourselves," a California brother says, offering us a rolled up bill.

"No thanks, man. I'll stick to this." I lift my bottle, smiling.

Jack's brows raise at the same time that he lifts his bottle to his lips. "It's been a while since I've seen you take a hit. I can drive us to the hotel if you want to let loose, you know that."

"No, I know." I shake my head. "I just don't really want to, I guess."

I take another drink, scanning the room as the front door opens and a group of girls walk in.

I turn my head away to talk to Jack when he bolts up from the couch, his eyes wide. "Sam?"

A girl from the group stops, her long brunette hair flying through the air as her head snaps toward us. "Jack?" Her face pales.

"What are you doing here?" he snaps, stepping closer to her. I stand up on instinct, keeping behind him.

She looks around, her arms crossing over her shirt that barely covers her tits and stomach. She looks young, or shit, younger than us.

"I... What are you?" She shakes her head, looking around the living room.

"She's underage," Jack announces, turning to the nearest California brother.

Everyone in the living room stops what they're doing when hearing that, the room falling silent. One of the Cali brothers steps up to her and motions for the door, making sure to not accidentally touch her. We do illegal shit hourly, but we don't party with underage girls.

"Jack!" she shouts. "You have to talk to me!"

He glares at her, and I watch, completely engrossed. "Get out, Sam," he says evenly, ignoring her.

Her eyes fill with tears. "Jack," she pleads.

"Get out, Sam," his voice takes on a warning tone and I step closer to him, standing alert. I've never heard him sound like this.

Her mouth hangs open helplessly as the brother finally gives her a gentle prod and she goes to the door, never looking away from Jack.

And he never looks away from her.

The door shuts behind her, but he stays in his place.

"Hey." I nudge his shoulder. Everyone else goes back to what they were doing before the small commotion. "Let's get out of here."

He nods, and I lay my arm over his shoulders to guide him through the back door, grabbing a bottle of vodka, and down the narrow walkway.

Cement gives way to sand as we walk onto the deserted beach. The moon reflects off of the wide open ocean and lights the pale sand beneath our boots.

We walk close to the water's edge, the crashing of the waves soothing, and take a seat on the sand.

"Who was that?" I cut to the chase. There's no need for pleasantries between us.

"Someone from my old life." He stares ahead, lifting the bottle to his lips.

Another wave comes in, almost brushing the toes of our leather boots. "Was she important?"

He takes a long drink, but I wait him out. "She was the only important one."

"Why didn't you talk to her?" I ask.

He turns to me, holding out to the bottle. "Why haven't you claimed Reyna?"

Grinning, I take the bottle and take a swig. "Fuck you, we're talking about you."

"And I'm done talking about me. Let's talk about you." Jack faces forward again.

Shaking my head, I set the bottle in the sand and drag it back and forth, creating a little hole for it to sit in. "Alright, I get it, asshole." I let out a deep sigh. "I don't know... There's so much more to her than I know."

Wyatt's giant ass plops down in the sand beside me, Mase on his other side. "So much more to who?"

"His Old Lady," Jack answers for me.

"What?" Wyatt's head snaps to me.

I shake my head. "I don't have an Old Lady."

"Might as well," Mason chimes in. "He hasn't looked at another girl since she showed up."

"She moved in with him," Jack adds, and I want to shove sand down his throat.

"I've been gone for two months!" Wyatt exclaims.

I take a drink to keep me from murdering these annoying fucks. "It's not what it sounds like."

"You like her?" Wyatt asks, his head inclining. I don't answer, because... I guess I haven't come to terms with what that means yet. "Holy shit." Wyatt's eyes soften and his mouth relaxes. "Make her your Old Lady when you're ready, but don't waste time. You don't know when it'll run out." I nod. I don't know what to say. "Promise me," he pushes.

"I promise," I agree. "But only if you promise us something first."

Wyatt grins, his white teeth shining in the moonlight. "What, you little shit?"

"Promise us you're happy here. That you're living again."

A somber look falls over Wyatt's weathered face, but slowly, he smiles again. Not the same one from before, but still a smile. "I'm happy here. The sun, the water, it's a good salve for regret and grief. The brothers have been good to me. They've taken me in without any pause."

"We miss you, Wyatt," Jacks says, bringing tears to Wyatt's eyes. It means a world more that it came from Jack.

"I miss you guys, too." He looks between the three of us. "But I can't come back."

"We know," Mason comes back in. "But never forget that you always have a home in Merrill Hill."

27

REYNA

HUNTLEY LEANS AGAINST THE OPPOSITE SIDE OF THE COUCH AS ME, her knees bent and a blanket resting over her legs. We're mirroring each other, relaxing on her couch in her living room, drinking wine, while her midnight black guard dogs rests on the floor at her side. That's something I've noticed since I got here yesterday. Noctem is always near. She sits by her feet while Huntley cooks and lies on the floor when we sit in the living room. Huntley said she lays outside of the shower while she bathes and she is on the bed at Huntley's feet when she sleeps.

I was a little frightened at first, scared the dog was going to snap at me if I got too close to Huntley, but Huntley said she didn't consider me a threat so she's calm.

This house is a far cry from Leo's cabin, though, I realized. A security alarm that says which doors are opening, cameras everywhere outside, and even a giant gun cabinet, bigger than me, in the master bedroom, plus the scary dog. It's clear Finn and Huntley do not take their safety lightly.

Leo, on the other hand, I'm not even sure he locks his front door when leaving the cabin. He certainly doesn't have cameras and a security system.

"You're joking," Huntley deadpans.

I shake my head, taking the last sip from my glass. "I'm not."

"You've never been to a party before," she repeats what I just said and I nod. Because I just said that. "That will not do." She looks around the dim house. "We're going to one. Go get ready."

Leo flits through my mind. I haven't heard from him since yesterday, and I have no idea when he's coming back, or what he's doing, or who he's with, or even why he left to begin with. And a large part of me wants him to feel the same way. I've also never gotten ready and gone out with a friend before, or really just did something because I enjoyed it. Everything I've ever done has always had some sort of motive. I shopped because I needed clothes and lingerie for work. I got beauty treatments for work. I got tattoos because I didn't want to look like the other girls at work who had minimal or no tattoos. Nothing I've ever done has just been for fun.

After showering, I join Huntley in her bathroom, where we stand side by side and do our makeup in the large mirror above the sinks.

Huntley pulls on a cropped tee shirt and high-waisted distressed boyfriend jeans with nude heels.

I examine her outfit before going back to my room and picking something out for myself. What do I wear to a college party? I choose a black, cropped tank top with the middle completely open and only held together by four gold chains and a pair of high-waisted, black, distressed jeans with black heeled boots.

We both top our outfits with our leather jackets and Huntley tells Noctem goodbye with a kiss on the head before we step into the garage and get into her shiny Jaguar.

Huntley parks a few houses down, but it's apparent which house we're going to the minute we step out of the car. There are a few people mingling in the yard, every window is lit up with light and the music can be heard from the road.

"Do you know these people?" I ask, staying by her side as we walk through the damp grass to the porch.

"Kinda. This house always has parties, especially this close to Halloween." She loops her arm in mine and it makes me feel a little more comfortable.

"So you don't actually know anyone here?" I ask.

She purses her lips as we step onto the small porch. "I used to know the girl who lived here, but I don't know if she moved after graduating. I kind of graduated and got married, so I'm not in the party loop anymore," she snarks, a small smile on her red lips.

"Fake it till we make it?" I ask.

"Mhmm," she hums, reaching for the door and turning the knob.

The house is packed, and not a single person turns to look our way as we walk into the sparsely furnished living room.

Walking through the house, we find a large cooler in the kitchen with bottled alcohol, so we choose from those and toss the caps into the garbage can before focusing on a card game going on at the table.

It's just ending and someone gets up, leaving the seat empty.

"Do you wanna play?" a guy asks, shuffling the cards.

I glance at Huntley, and she nods, shoving me toward the table. I take a seat as the guy fans out the cards around a can of beer.

"What is this?" I ask, looking back at Huntley.

"Ring of Fire," the shuffling guy answers. "You both can play if you want."

Huntley places her arm over my shoulders and sits on one of my legs, and I naturally wrap my arm around her back to support her. She's light, but her ass is kind of boney.

"How do you play?" I ask, leaning closer to Huntley.

She turns to me. "You choose a card and each number has a different action you have to do. Once you've chosen your card, you stick it under the tab of the can. If it pops open with your card, you have to drink the beer, usually chugging it."

"Gross," I answer, scrunching my nose.

Huntley grins maliciously. "Welcome to a college party, babe."

We go around the table, choosing cards and doing their actions. I pull a two, so I get to choose a person to take a drink. I choose the girl across the table from Huntley and I. Huntley picks a seven, so everyone has to point to the sky and the last person to do it, drinks, which ends up being a guy to our left. We continue on and on, sliding the cards under the tab carefully, until I slide my card in—a six, so all guys had to drink—and I hear the quiet *hiss* of the tab popping.

"Shit," I sigh, and everyone around the table hoops and hollers.

The guy who shuffled, and seems to run the games, takes all the cards out from under the tab and finishes popping it before handing it to me. "Drink up," he laughs.

With a sigh, I take the can from him and try to chug it as quickly as possible. I hate the taste of beer, so it doesn't go down the easiest, but once it's done, I slam it on the table and quickly pick up my vodka mixer to wash it down.

The combination of the two is almost worse than the beer by itself, but Huntley's laugh and smile pull me back into the moment and I realize that I'm having fun. *Real* fun.

We play a few more rounds before excusing ourselves to get another drink and explore the rest of the house. Luckily, I don't lose any more, and somehow Huntley made it out unscathed every time.

We step into the garage. The only lights are the flashing

LEDs and party lights, and the song "Drugs & Money" by Chase Atlantic bleeds into here as well. There's a long table set up in the middle of the one-car garage, and Huntley and I watch one game of beer pong before she's volunteering us for the next round.

I suck, and Huntley's not much better. We're easily being beaten by a team of two young guys, and when their ball circles our last cup, Huntley and I both dart down to blow it out of the cup, knocking heads in the process. We both straighten, holding the sides of our foreheads and laughing, the guys across the table laughing at our expense too.

Huntley and I drain the rest of our drinks as is customary to do as the loser, apparently, and make our way back inside for a refill.

"I haven't had to call my dad to pick me up from a party since I was a freshman. He's gonna love this," she laughs.

"What about your car?" I sway a little, the continuous chugging getting to me. Normally, I only sip champagne before a client and I head upstairs, or stay in the lounges, whatever they're into.

Huntley shrugs, smiling wide. "We can come back and get it tomorrow. This is a safe neighborhood. I used to leave my car here a lot when I partied here as a freshman. Let's go get another drink and go to the bathroom. I have to pee."

I loop my arm in Huntley's as we walk back into the house and into the kitchen, grab a new bottle each, and then through the living room and into a narrow hallway where she goes into the bathroom. I lean against the wall and wait for her, putting the bottle to my lips and taking a long drink. I like this feeling. The weightlessness, the lack of caring about anything. I just want to enjoy myself and have fun with Huntley. She's really great. And oh my god, she's beautiful. She could have been a serious competitor at La Lujuria.

"Hey," a brunette guy says, leaning against the opposite wall. He kind of looks like Leo. the longer hair on top, even though his is shorter, and he has it styled wrong, and his lips aren't nearly as full as Leo's... and his eyes are all wrong, but he's close enough, I guess.

I cock my head to the side, my eyes running down his slightly muscular body. Leo's is better. "Hey." I smile flirtatiously. I can't help it. If Leo's not here, then he'll do.

"Do you want a little boost?" he asks, opening his palm and revealing a small white pill.

"What is it?" I ask, stepping closer to him, accidentally bumping his chest with mine, as I get too close.

He leans down to my ear and whispers, "Molly."

Inclining my head to look at him, I nod, smiling. *Why the hell not?* I take the pill out of his offered hand and put it on my tongue as the bathroom door opens, and use my drink to wash it down.

"What the fuck did you just give her?" Huntley shouts, moving me out of the way.

Stumble back into the wall, hitting my back hard as Huntley cocks her fist back and punches the knock off Leo in his face.

"You fucking bitch!" he shouts, and then I realize that the entire house is louder than it was a few minutes ago.

People run by, two girls shoving between Huntley and me and into the bathroom, the door slamming behind them.

In a rush of blue, I see a police officer take Huntley's arm and place them behind her back. *Oh shit.*

"It was both of them! That one is on something!" Leo lookalike points at me.

My eyes widen as another officer comes over to me. "What are you on?" he asks.

"Shut up, Reyna!" Huntley shouts, already being walked away in handcuffs.

I blink, keeping my mouth shut, and the officer sighs, "Come on, you can sober up with your friend."

"Why is she being arrested?" I ask, stepping forward as the officer places his hand on my shoulder and directs me to move.

"Assault, for punching that kid," he says evenly.

I look around as I'm marched through the house. Another two officers are checking the IDs of everyone in the living room and kitchen. I'd bet those two girls who rushed into the bathroom are underage. I hope they were at least able to get out through a window or something.

The cool night air smacks me in the face as we walk out of the house, and I feel a bit of my brain return to me as some of the alcohol fog clears, but not a lot.

White hair flies through the air as Huntley snaps her head around and she purses her lips as she sees me walking toward her.

The officer opens the back door and leads Huntley inside, and waits there until my officer and I reach the car and he nudges me to go in as well.

Huntley scoots over and I take her seat while the police close the door.

"Is your dad still going to love picking us up from the police station?" I ask, trying to bring some light to the situation. I don't know what's going to happen when we get to the police station. I don't have any form of ID. Are they going to book us?

"Fuck no, I'll call Randy." She moves around, her arms still stuck behind her.

"Who's that?" I rest my hands in my lap, feeling sorry for Huntley's arms.

She sighs, settling back as much as she can. "My father-in-law."

The officers get into the front seats and start the car. Dropping my head against the seat, I close my eyes. There isn't anything I can do now.

I don't know how long we drive for. I lose perception of time as the molly kicks in and I feel warmth rise from my lower belly and the alcohol fog coming back, but I suppose it's more of a drug fog now.

My body feels weightless and I feel like I'm rocking in a pool of water, the flow of it knocking me back and forth gently. I just feel good. Light and warm.

In the back of my mind, I hear the loud rumbling of Leo's bike, and I think about him. Why didn't he take me with him? Will he pick me up from the police station?

The police cruiser slams to a stop and Huntley and I jolt forward, the seat belt cutting into the side of my neck as it locks up with the force.

"What the fuck?" one officer says.

"God-fucking-dammit. I'm so tired of these Outlaws running this fucking town," another groans. And Huntley laughs manically in response.

Both back doors rip open, and I turn to see Leo's eyes shining in the moonlight. He braces one tan arm on the roof of the SUV cruiser and leans down, a black bandana covering his nose and mouth and the lower part of his face. "What did you get yourself into, Siren?"

"You handcuffed my Old Lady?" Finn snarls.

"She punched someone," the driver says quickly.

"Keys. Right fucking now."

I can't look away from Leo. He offers his hand and I take it, stepping out of the police car and walking with him toward his bike that's parked in front of the police car.

Leo looks back at me and stops abruptly.

With his hand on my chest, he pushes me against the cop car, my back bending backward over the hood.

He keeps his hand pressing me into the car, and his other hand takes my chin in his grip, holding me still. Leo leans in close and stares into my eyes, his narrowing; his bandana brushes under my chin. "What the fuck did you take?"

Without thinking, I arch my back, my breasts pushing into Leo's chest. "Molly."

He shakes his head, pushing off of me. "Fucking hell, Reyna. Do you know what kind of shit people could cut with molly?"

He yanks my hand, jerking me off of the car and pulling me toward his bike. Finn and Huntley are already sitting on his, next to Leo's.

Leo gets on and waits for me. "Can you hold on long enough to get home?" he asks as I sit down behind him.

"I think so," I answer hesitantly.

He shakes his head again. "Tap my shoulder if you feel like you're gonna pass out."

He waves to Finn and guns the engine the second my arms wrap around his stomach.

28

REYNA

GOOD NEWS, I MADE IT TO THE CABIN WITHOUT FALLING OFF THE bike and dying. But the rumbling of the bike made my legs fall asleep.

Leo turns the key on the bike and the roaring stops immediately, the engine turning off. We sit in the pitch black darkness, the only light being the moon high in the sky. "Do you need help?" Leo finally asks.

"I think so," I answer. If I weren't impaired, I'd feel ashamed.

He chuckles. "Hold on to my shoulders so you don't fall when I get off. I'll carry you." I place one hand on Leo's shoulder while he sets the bike down and swings his leg over. As soon as he turns around, I'm already reaching for him. He catches me as I almost fall off of the bike, my legs wrapping around his waist, and my arms around his shoulders tightly. "Well, okay then."

"You said you were going to carry me," I state, resting my forehead against my arm.

"I did. I just didn't expect you to pounce on me." His large hands cradle my ass, and I don't say a word in fear that he'll move them.

I lift my head slightly, trying to look into his hazel eyes that I missed tonight. "You don't want to be close to me?"

"I've been dying to get between your legs, Siren." He smirks and heat floods me. The light click of the front door unlocking reaches me and I lift myself up, grinding against Leo's stomach, staring into his eyes. "No," he groans, his fingers digging into the denim covering my ass. "Don't do this to me." His head drops backward, his eyes squeezing closed.

"Do what?" I ask, leaning forward and nibbling a line up his exposed neck to his ear.

"This is just the molly, Siren. It'll be over soon and you'll go back to teasing me," he grits out between his teeth.

"No, it's not. I've wanted you for weeks, but playing with you is fun." I grin, lifting myself to grind against him again.

My back lands on a bed—and after a quick look around, I realize it's my bed—and Leo kneels between my open legs with one knee.

"It's the molly, babe," he says quietly against my lips.

"You know you want me." I move my head from side to side, letting my lips brush against his.

His eyes close, but he stays right here. "I really fucking do, but I can't fuck you when you're on this shit."

I wrap my arms around his neck and hold him to me, making sure he can't leave. I'm getting what I want tonight. "Please, Leo."

"Tomorrow when you're sober," he counters.

"I need you tonight. If you don't fuck me, I'll have to take care of myself and it'll be such a waste." I pout. "Please," I drag out the word, begging.

"I can't fuck you," he says again and I pull him to my face, cutting off whatever else he's going to say by kissing him.

He immediately complies. His teeth biting into my bottom lip and pulling it before letting it go. His mouth attacks mine with so much passion it overwhelms me. My entire body feels like it lights up. Like my body was set on fire and everything is burning. I moan into his mouth, surprising myself. Kissing has never turned me on, but I'm flooded already and he hasn't even touched me.

Leo pulls away, his hands sliding down my sides. The heat of his hands burn into my skin almost painfully. Every touch is so intense, so sensual. "But I can make you come to take the edge off for tonight."

"You're so confident," I snark, excited that he's finally giving in to me.

"Siren, this is what I'm best at." He smirks, and I feel another rush flow straight to my pussy.

The moonlight shines into my room, shining on the side of Leo's face and enhancing his already sharp jawline.

His long fingers skillfully unbutton my jeans and drag them down my legs before tossing them and my boots on the floor, and I clumsily tear off my leather jacket, ditching it as well.

He reaches down, his thumb sliding over my clit while he leans down and kisses my neck. The lace of my panties creates a friction that feels so good.

"How many times are you going to come for me, Siren?" he asks, his voice rough and sexy.

I moan as his thumb quickens, rubbing up and down before he slides them aside and slowly slides two fingers inside of me. They glide in easily with how wet I am. He pumps a few times before bringing his soaked fingers out and rubbing them over my clit again. I buck my hips, wanting him back inside of me.

"Oh, you want to ride, baby? Ride my face then." He smiles and stands from the bed.

I rise to my elbows at the loss of him and watch as he pulls his shirt over his head and drops it to the floor next to my clothes.

Leo takes my hand and guides me to stand before taking my place on the bed.

"Come on, Siren. Climb up." He settles himself on a pillow and looks at me.

As stable as possible, I crawl up the bed and over his body before swinging my leg over his face and hovering there, holding onto the headboard for balance.

"Nope," he says quickly, placing his hands on the tops of my thighs and pushing me onto his face.

My eyes widen as he eats me out. His tongue dips into my pussy before sweeping up and massaging my clit, and he does this repeatedly.

When I think my head is going to explode from just that, he sucks my clit into his mouth, hard, like he's trying to suck it through a straw. The noises that leave my body are foreign and so blissful. I start to really ride his face, moving my hips back and forth while he sucks on my clit.

He lets it go with a loud slurping noise and flattens his tongue for me to grind against.

His tongue hits everything. It dips inside of me, slides through my folds, and presses against my clit with just enough pressure to have me quicken my pace, chasing an orgasm so strong, I know it's going to fuck me up. One of Leo's hands leaves my thigh and slides up my stomach and under my crop top, where he rolls my nipple between his finger and thumb, and like a switch, it triggers a hurricane of an orgasm.

My entire body jolts and twitches as it passes through me, and for a moment I think I might lose consciousness, but finally it passes, and I can feel Leo's tongue lightly lapping at my pussy.

I fall off of him and onto my back beside him; every muscle in my body is spent.

An overwhelming wave of exhaustion falls over me, but the last thing I see before my eyes close is Leo turning over to look at me, his entire mouth and chin glistening in the moonlight.

29

LEO

Reyna's ink black hair fans out over the white pillowcase. Her chest falls and rises slowly as she sleeps deeply. I stayed up the entire night to watch her and be sure she didn't have a negative reaction to the drug. I can't believe she took drugs from someone she didn't know. Shouldn't she know better than that? She worked in the party industry. I'm sure dudes were snorting all kinds of shit before getting their rocks off on that island.

How did I not know there was an illegal sex club right off the coast of Seattle? Those are two of my favorite pastimes: sex and illegal things.

My eyes water as I yawn for the millionth time. After driving nine hours, receiving the call that Huntley and Reyna were arrested, rushing to them with Finn, and then staying awake to ensure Reyna didn't die in her sleep, I'm pretty fucking beat.

Not to mention finally getting to taste Reyna's pussy. Fucking hell, that was the highlight of my fucking life.

I need coffee.

Rolling over, I climb out of Reyna's bed and walk to the door. I'll just brew some coffee and come right back in. She'll most likely need some when she wakes up, anyway.

But I stop short when I see her duffle bag sitting on the floor by the door. It's unzipped and her hairbrush lies on top.

That would be perfect for Mason. But if I took it now, would she know when it went missing?

I'm standing in the doorway debating this when Reyna stirs behind me in her bed.

"What are you doing?" she asks groggily.

"I was going to make some coffee," I answer, turning around.

She's propped up on her elbow, rubbing her eyes. Her crop top is only covering one tit, and fuck me, I want to suck the exposed one into my mouth.

She stops messing with her eye and catches me staring. "I didn't forget last night." She smirks.

"How could you? I'm unforgettable."

Reyna shakes her head, pausing on the side of the bed where I stayed all night. "Did you sleep in here?" She turns back to me, cocking her head.

I bite my lip, playing out what to say. I can't say I watched her all night. That's fucking creepy. "Someone had to make sure you didn't suffocate in your sleep." I raise my eyebrow, challenging her.

"Coffee?" she asks, changing the subject.

Nodding, I turn around to leave the room, my eyes glossing over the hairbrush again. Not right now, but that's what I'm taking.

Reyna curls up on the couch with a blanket and the TV volume on low, and I approach her with a tall glass of water.

"Keep drinking water. I'll be back in a few hours." I set the glass on the coffee table and pull my keys out of my cut pocket.

"Where are you going?" She raises her head, black strands of hair fall into her face, but she leaves them, not bothering to push them back.

"To Finn's, to see how much trouble we're in for busting you and Huntley out." I cross my arms over my chest. The leather under my arms feels like home. I'll wear this cut until the day I die.

Reyna smiles and I have the feeling that she's not at all ashamed of last night. Not any part of it.

———

MY BIKE TIRES hit the smooth concrete of Evans Body Shop, and I park in front of one of the open bays. I won't be here long.

Finn rolls out from under a classic Corvette, eyeing me as I walk into the shop.

"Your girls a bad influence on my Old Lady." Finn rises to sit on the creeper and wipes his hands off on a worn red rag.

I prop my ass against a metal table along the wall, crossing my arms. "I'm pretty sure your Old Lady was the one in hand-cuffs for assault."

Finn smirks, shaking his head. "I'm surprised it took her this long to get picked up for that shit. She thinks she's a street fighter."

I chuckle, because he's fucking right, but Huntley isn't just talk. She will take on anyone and I'd bet my money on her every time. "She could beat my ass."

Finn barks a loud laugh. "Mine too, she's scrappy."

Our laughter settles down. "So, should we call Robinson and clear everything up?" We might run this town, but we can't just take our girls out of a cop cage with no push back. The pigs have to at least *look* like they have us under control.

Finn shakes his head, standing and grabbing a water bottle from the table I'm standing against. "Nah. I already talked to him. They were just going to release them anyway, so we saved them a phone call."

Nodding, I laugh under my breath. "Those two together are going to be dangerous."

"Yeah," Finn agrees. "But I haven't seen her this happy with another woman. She loves Reese and Allie, but they already had each other, ya know? She kind of felt like a third wheel."

"I could see that. Reese and Allie are really close and they've known each other since college." I look around, realizing my little buddy hasn't come to greet me yet. "Is Huntley in this morning?"

Finn grins. "No, *Noctem* and Huntley are at home, sleeping off Huntley's hangover. I know you actually mean her."

I shrug. He caught me. "She's my niece. Of course I want to see her." I stretch my arms over my head as a few of Finn's new employees trickle into the shop and head to the office to put their lunches in the fridge. Even though I didn't love working on cars, I still enjoyed working here with Finn and Jack, and I kind of miss it. "Must be nice to get to stay home when you have a hangover."

"Yeah, I think she's fucking the boss," Finn says with a dead serious face, which just makes me laugh even harder.

"Alright," I sigh. "I need to get back so I can finish my bathroom before the Halloween party tonight."

"Fuck." Finn drags his hand over his face. "Yeah, that's tonight."

"You excited, big boy?" I tease, waggling my brows.

He looks up at the ceiling before answering, like gods gonna fucking save him from this. *Fat chance, brother.* "Yes and no. Huntleys going to look fucking sexy up on stage, but I don't know how I'll do with other guys watching her."

"You'll be fine. If anyone's got the patience for that, it's you." I smile.

"How do you do it every weekend?" he asks, cocking his head.

"Reynas not my girl," I answer.

Finn narrows his eyes. "If she weren't your girl, you wouldn't have stopped her from dancing on customers, so you wanna try that again?"

"No," I say honestly and turn around to leave. "See you tonight, brother!" I call out, waving my hand in the air as I walk toward my bike.

The truth is, I enjoy watching Reyna on stage too much to be upset over her being up there. It feels good to know the woman who every man in that club wants, wants me.

30

—

REYNA

I PACE BACK AND FORTH IN THE LOCKER ROOM, WAITING FOR Huntley. I don't know why I'm feeling nervous about this set. Yes, it's a little different from my other routines, but it's hot as hell and Huntley and I have drilled this routine into our brains, so there isn't a chance we can make a mistake.

Finally, Huntley walks through the door, a large tote bag slung over her shoulder. Her white blonde hair hangs in loose curls down her back, and her face is free of makeup.

"I'm so excited." Her eyes widen with glee, and it's enough to make the bundle of anxiety in my stomach completely dissipate.

I chuckle and loop my arm through one of hers and we walk to the wall of vanities together. We find two open seats next to each other and sit down to do our makeup together.

I really enjoy it. I like watching how Huntley does her makeup, and how different yet similar our styles are. How different they look on both of us. Huntley is all sharp features and classic looks. Winged liner, natural lashes, and red lipstick. Where I like big false lashes, deep red lips, and dark contour so I can have half the cheekbones that Huntley has.

Leo opens the door, calling out one of the dancer's names. I watch him, leaning into the room, keeping the door close to his body so no one can see into the room.

His eyes scan the small group of women rushing around the locker room and finally stop on me. His lips slowly slide into a smirk and he winks before backing out and closing the door.

Huntley's head swivels toward me, her mouth open in a wide grin. "Took you two long enough."

"Ugh, shut up," I groan, leaning closer to the magnifying mirror to line my lips.

"Please don't hurt him." Her tone turns somber. "Because then I'd have to kick your ass, and I like you too much to want to do that."

"It's not serious between us," I lie. "No one is going to end up hurt."

Huntley turns back to the mirror. "Whatever you say." The music switches in the main room and increases slightly. "Are we not opening tonight?" Huntley asks.

"No, Leo switched the spots, and we're kind of the main act." I prop my leg up on the table and rub a baby wipe over it to get the lotion off.

"Oh, okay!" Huntley swipes a wipe from my pack and does the same thing.

We change into our costumes. Huntley wears a bright white corset and thong with white, thigh-high leather stripper boots and a pair of wings strapped to her back. With her soft white curls, she looks... heavenly. Ya know, if heaven had strippers. I'm dressed almost the opposite to her. I have the same corset but in black, with the matching thong in red, and my black, open-toed, stripper heels with the glitter jack-o'-lantern face on them, and I put a headband in my hair with two red devil horns on it.

I'm putting hair oil on the ends of my pin-straight hair when

Jack walks into the room, his blonde hair hanging in his brooding eyes. "Reyna, Huntley!" he calls. This man is too grumpy for how many strippers throw themselves at him every week.

"Ready?" I ask, smirking.

Huntley licks her matte lips and nods. "Hell yeah." *That's my girl.*

We walk to the stage together and get into position before the song starts.

I lay on the floor in front of Huntley on my side, and she lies on her stomach. When "Goosebumps" by Travis Scott starts, I push up onto my shoulders, upside down, and hold my legs open. The toes of my heels almost touch the floor, and Huntley crawls toward me, sliding her hands down the inside of my thighs as I sway back and forth. She pulls back, sticking one leg straight into the air as I drop onto my back and sit up.

As we transition into the next move, I glance around at the crowd. The chairs are back in front of my stage, but probably because Leo knows there won't be any lap dances in this routine. But he's front and center next to Finn, who looks pissed and enthralled all at once. Money is already littering the stage, covering it almost completely.

Huntley and I line up, facing each other, and intertwined our legs—her sitting over mine—we look into each other's eyes, and I lean forward and lick up her cheek. I barely hear her sharp intake of breath over the music, and I smirk. We didn't plan that, whoops.

The crowd cheers, and money rains down on the stage. Predictable.

Huntley moves to the pole, and climbs to the top, swinging around and tossing her hair as she goes while I move to my knees and bounce my ass, waiting for her to get to her spot.

Once she's there, I crawl to the pole as well and climb about to the middle. Huntley held an inverted split while I was climbing, but when she sees me, she pulls her legs together and we move around the pole until we're at opposite sides and she slides down so we're in a sixty-nine position and she wraps her arms around my waist.

With my legs wrapped around the pole, I let go with my hands and lean backward while Huntley lets go with her legs and bends backward as well.

She slinks down the pole while I climb up, and the rest is just us mirroring each other. Huntley inverts at the bottom of the pole and opens her legs in a straddle, and I do the same at the top, but I stay upright. We spin around the pole and as Huntley wraps her legs around the pole again, using her hand under her butt to hold her in place, her body long as she lays flat, her back toward the floor. While she did that, I spread my legs out over the pole and held them in a middle split against the pole.

When she's in position, I wrap my legs around the pole and slide down quickly until I'm hovering over her like we practiced that first day in the studio.

The crowd loses their minds again, the cheering deafening as I use my arms to pump myself up and down on top of her.

Huntley drops one leg to the floor, her ass next and then slides away from the pole, holding one leg in the air so I can get down too.

She moves to her hands and knees, and I crawl up behind her and lay down over her back as the song fades out.

Huntley's back rises and falls rapidly and I push off of her so we can both get up.

She takes my offered hand, and we let the security sweep up the money that covers the stage. Good thing we did floor work at the beginning. We would have been slipping all over the stage if we did the floor work after the pole work.

Huntley pulls me into a hug at the bottom of the stairs, and not even her sweat covered chest could make me push her away. I had a lot of fun dancing with her. To get to interact and catch glimpses of her on stage while we were dancing was heartwarming. To do something together, something we both enjoy; it was great.

Leo's hand wraps around my arm, and he walks me through the crowd. Huntley stops at Finn and drops onto his lap and I turn to Leo. "Wait, I need to talk to you."

"About what? We can talk in the locker room," he yells over the music.

"No. Right now." I pull out of his grip and take his hand instead, leading him to one of the VIP lounges.

I drag Leo into the lounge and yank the curtains closed behind us.

"Siren, people might think naughty things about us," Leo mocks.

Turning around, I start unhooking my corset. "Then they'd be right."

He places his hands on my wrists, stopping me as my tits spill from the unhooked corset. "Reyna. I can't continue being a good guy and turning you down."

I pull my wrists from his hands and place them on his chest, pushing him toward the half circle leather couch.

"I don't want a good guy, pet. I want everything you've been holding back from me." Leo's calves hit the couch and he bends to sit.

"I'm not your *pet* then," he enunciates the name. "I'm not one of your clients."

"Okay," I agree. He's right, he's so much more. I finish unhooking the corset and drop it to the floor at my feet.

"On your knees, Siren." His eyes fall to my breasts while I comply with his orders. "Take out my cock and show me what you can do."

I unzip his jeans and pull them down his hips with his boxers, freeing his cock. His thick, long, smooth cock.

Dicks aren't an attractive body part, but this one? This one is a work of art.

Bending forward, I spit on his dick and use my hand to rub it in, getting it nice and wet. I squeeze his thick cock as I jerk him off and then I take him in my mouth, hollowing my cheeks so I can suck him hard.

Leo gathers my hair off of my face and holds it behind my head, his fist resting heavily on my head.

He sucks in a harsh breath when I swirl my tongue around his head and tickle the little strip of skin under the head.

"Can you take all of me?" he asks, his eyes zeroing in on my mouth around cock.

If I could smile, I would. I relax my cheeks and throat, and start to take him down my throat.

When I get to the bottom of his dick, Leo says, "That's it, Reyna. I'm gonna fuck your throat now." His hand on my head takes over, and he guides me up and down his cock, my nose brushing against the skin of his pelvis.

With my hands free, I move his balls around in the palm of my hand, then lightly squeeze. Leo jumps about an inch off the couch, his cock shoving even further into my throat.

"Fuck, Siren. You're done, ride me." He releases my hair and I get to my feet. I place my hands on his shoulders and straddle Leo's lap. "Nah, nah, nah, nah," he rushes out. "I don't want your pretty pussy covered up. I want to see it take me."

The thin material slides down my legs and crumples to the floor next to my corset.

With my legs on either side of Leo's thighs, I hover over his dick for a moment. Our eyes lock, and it hits me—harder than I expected. I'm about to fuck someone just because I want to. Not because he paid me.

And I sink down on his thick, long cock, enjoying every second of the stretch. Leo's head drops to the back of the couch and his hands grip my ass.

"Fuck, you feel fucking perfect," Leo sighs.

I roll my hips in a figure eight motion, slowly at first. My hands rest on Leo's shoulders and my tits brush against Leo as I move.

My sensitive nipples brush over the soft leather and harsh zipper of Leo's cut, sending zings up my spine and straight down to my clit. A moan falls out of my mouth.

"Mmm," Leo hums. "Sing for me, Siren."

Leo's hands on my ass push me, urging me to move faster and faster until finally Leo has taken full control as he bounces me on his dick quickly.

His head comes forward and takes one of my nipples in his mouth, and now I drop my head back, enjoying the sensations of the rough zipper, his wet mouth, and his yummy cock in my pussy.

This is amazing.

I don't want to admit that having feelings for someone really does make the sex better, but this is damn near mind blowing.

I don't know if I can go back to having sex with clients after being fucked like this.

Leo pulls me off of his dick, one of his hands moving to my lower back so he can lay me down.

As soon as my back and Leo's knees hit the couch, he's already plunging back into me. I don't even get to breathe—not that I want to.

Leo is... smooth is the only way I can describe him. The way he moves his hips, gliding to hit spots inside of me that only I have ever been able to find.

His hips don't stutter or slow. He's measured and precise and just... smooth.

One of his arms holds himself up against the back of the couch, and he moves the other to my clit, his thumb gently making circles around the sensitive button.

"I can feel you, Siren, you're close." I moan loudly. He's right. My vision is already starting to black out around the edges.

My eyes flutter closed and I reach between us and place my finger over Leo's thumb, applying more pressure to my clit.

"I'm taking you home and fucking you again so you better not pass out on me, Reyna," Leo growls, his hips picking up pace. With every thrust, my body scoots along the couch, but Leo follows me, not letting me get a single second of reprieve from the overwhelming sensations.

Until finally, my pleasure crests and my orgasm hits me like a tsunami wave, and it doesn't just hit once. The ripples feel like several more orgasms, one right after the other. All of my muscles lock up and my thighs tremble with the force of my orgasm.

"Jesus fuck," Leo grunts, his hips finally stuttering as he just pounds into me without any smooth movement to him.

I swear I can feel him in my throat when he comes deep inside of me.

I can already feel his absence as he pulls out of me and kneels between my legs, staring down at me.

He stands, pulling up his jeans, and I take that as my cue to leave as well.

Leo watches me as I hook my corset together and licks his lips.

He shrugs out of his cut and hands it to me. "Here, wear this."

"Why?" I ask, eyeing the black leather vest.

His eyes darken. "So that when we walk out of here, everyone knows that you're mine."

"Am I?" I cock my head, my straight hair tickling my hip.

"Yeah, you fucking are." It almost sounds like a threat. And I love it.

31

LEO

Reyna turns her back to me, and when I don't move, she looks over her shoulder.

Taking the hint, I step forward and drape my cut over her slender shoulders.

The corner of her maroon lips lifts in a smirk, and it does something to me. Seeing her in my cut does something to me. It triggers something possessive and primal in me. Something I've never experienced. Fucking her without a condom doesn't help the fact, either. I haven't done that shit since I first had sex in high school; the few times I tempted fate before I wised the fuck up. We're fine though. Reyna was a sex worker, so she's definitely clean and I'm sure she's still on her birth control. There's no fucking way La Lujuria was letting their girls walk around without getting tested regularly and without some sort of birth control.

Everything with Reyna is something I've never experienced. And I'm learning to be less afraid every time my stomach flutters and ties into a knot.

But I have to do one thing before I can really feel comfortable with her, and she might hate me if she finds out.

I tuck Reyna under my arm and walk her to the locker room. People's heads turn and watch us, and I feel so much pride in this moment. They all know she's mine.

I hold the locker room door open for Reyna and watch her ass sway as she walks in. Fuck, maybe we should have round two in the showers.

"I just need to change and freshen up and I can work the floor." Reyna unlocks her locker and pulls her LV duffle out.

"No dances, just talking," I warn her.

She rolls her eyes, but smiles, so I know she's not upset. "Yes, sir."

I eye her bag as she digs around, finding a new outfit. *Please leave it out, please leave it out, please...*

Yes! Reyna leaves her bag sitting on the bench as she walks to one of the changing stalls.

As quietly as possible, I walk to her bag and shuffle a few things aside before I find her hairbrush.

I almost sprint to the door, trying to get out of here before she's done changing. "Hey, Jack needs me, but I'll be watching you out there," I yell, pulling the door open and slipping out before she can reply.

In Jack and I's office, I seal the hairbrush in a ziplock bag and hope that's enough for Mase to get some sort of ID on her.

And then my gaze catches on my jeans.

I yank open the drawers on the desk. I know I saw Q-Tips in here the other day. Loudly, I search through the drawers, shoving things out of the way and tossing them out when I finally find the Q-Tips.

Shoving my pants down quickly, I glance at the door. This is going to be so weird if someone were to walk in right now.

I twirl the cotton swab over my cock, hopefully getting it nice and soaked in Reyna's saliva and cum, and I toss that into a second sealed bag and pull up my pants. Good thing I brought more than one.

The office door swings open, startling me as I shove the hairbrush and Q-Tip in my back pocket.

Cale peeks his head in. "Hey, there's a fight out front."

Grinning, I bite my lip. "Nothing like a fight after busting a nut."

Cale and I run out of the office and through the club to the front door, shoving people aside as we go, but most everybody is already looking toward the front doors where there is indeed a commotion.

Finn already has one guy restrained as Jack struggles with the other. He's putting up a hell of a fight, but I'm not too proud to fight somebody two on one if he's fucking around in my place of business.

I grab the guy's shirt at the shoulders and yank him away from Jack and toward the floor, where I follow him down and lay into his face with my fist. Okay, only a few punches. I still have to be somewhat professional.

I push off of him and Jack kneels down to grab the front of his shirt, and together we lift him to his feet. Saint and Mason finally come over to see what's going on.

Finn shoves the guy he had a hold of through the front door, the guy's lip bleeding in the corner.

"Get the fuck out of my club, and if you come back in here again and start shit like this, you'll be banned for life, got it?" I push the guy's back and shove him through the front door as well.

Fuck them. If they want to finish their fight in the parking lot, then that's none of my business.

Looking around, I see Reyna standing outside of the locker room next to Huntley. Her dark hair falls in her face like a curtain.

"Hey, I'll be right back," I say to Jack, leaning closer to him so he can hear me.

He nods and I turn away from Reyna and grab Mason's arm, pulling him through the front door.

The cold air penetrates my body the moment I step outside. Jesus fuck, it's cold. My boots crunch over the loose gravel as we walk away from the club.

"Here." I grab the bags out of my back pocket and hand them to him. "I got her DNA."

He looks at the bags. "Her hair brush?" I nod. "A cheek swab? How did you get that?" His dark brows pull together. "Did you tell her?"

I shake my head, a proud grin pulling at my lips. "She gave me head, and I fucked her without a condom, so I swabbed my dick."

Mason's mouth drops open and he hands the bag with the Q-Tip back to me. "You can keep that."

"What? It won't work?" I ask.

Mase purses his lips. "I don't even want to find out. The brush will be enough."

I shrug. "If you say so." Tucking my hands in my jeans pockets, we walk back to the club, and I toss the baggy in the trash can by the door.

The rest of the night goes by without incident. Reyna walks around and talks to the customers, guys and girls alike, but she doesn't do more than talk to them, which is good. I'm sure she'd hate for me to bend her over my knee on stage and spank her in front of everyone. Or maybe she'd like it. There's so much for me to learn about her.

"Come on, Siren," I call to her at the end of the night.

She rolls her eyes as the other dancers' heads snap to stare at her, and I smirk, leaving her in the dressing room to get dressed. Is it the most mature thing to do? No. But I like the idea of the other girls knowing she's mine. I mean, they already had suspicions. They know we live together and that was enough to cross me off of their list, which I'm fine with. I never planned to fuck my strippers. Women don't always like my carefree ways, and the last thing we needed was someone quitting because they hated me.

Or stalking me.

Reyna steps out of the locker room, my cut slung over her shoulders on top of a hoodie and matching sweats.

"Quit staring at me," she sasses, walking past me toward the door.

"You don't want me to do that. You like being watched, I can tell." She scowls at me, and I know that I'm right. I step into her, placing my hands on her waist and pulling her into my body. "You enjoy being watched, don't you, Siren? Do you want me to watch as you play with your pretty pussy tonight?"

She pushes me away with a dainty hand on my chest. "All you think about is sex." She rolls her eyes.

"All I think about is you," I correct her. She bites the inside of her lip. And this is something I'm not used to. Reyna always has something to say. I like that I fluster her. "Let's go get some food." I sling my arm over her shoulder and lead her out to my Mustang.

"WHAT'S something you've always wanted to do?" I take a bite out of my burger, watching Reyna in the passenger's seat.

"Mmm," she hums, her dark lips wrapped around the straw of her milkshake. "Drive, I guess."

"You want to learn how to drive?" The dash lights shine on her perfect face.

"Yeah." She sets the paper cup in the cup holder. "I hate that if I ever needed to drive. I don't even know how."

Tossing my burger wrapper in the takeout bag, I open my door. "Switch me places. I'll teach you."

"What!? No!" She startles, her eyes widening.

I close the door, leaning toward her slightly. "You want to sit on my lap and learn, Siren?" Her head angles downward and she glances at me from under her lashes, nodding. "Climb on over then." I open my arms to welcome her.

She places one hand on my thigh and the other on the steering wheel as she climbs over the center console and into my lap.

I wrap my arms around her and take her hands in mine. Her cherry perfume slaps me in the face, and I place her hands on the steering wheel. "You can hold it wherever you're comfortable, but this is the placement you learn." She nods her head. "Touch the pedals with your right foot only." I pat her thigh with my hand. Her leg lifts off of mine as she explores. "The one on the left, the long one?"

"Uh huh." She nods.

"That's the brake. And the skinny one on the right is the gas."

"Okay." She looks down at the gearshift. "And this is the shifter," she states.

I nod behind her, but since she can't see, I also say, "Yes, the gearshift. P is for park, D is for drive—"

"I'm not stupid, Leo. I know what the letters stand for," she snaps, interrupting me.

I move my arms to her side and rub them up and down. "I never said you were, Siren. Don't put words in my mouth." She releases a breath, and I know she's calming down. "I'll get us out of the parking lot and onto the road and then you can take over, okay?"

She nods and I press my foot on the brake and back us out of our parking spot. The roads are deserted because of how late it is, and when I get us on the road, I let off of the gas and guide Reyna's hands to the wheel. "Just don't kill us, Siren."

"You're so encouraging," she snaps, her petite hands wrapping around the leather wheel, and she hesitantly presses the gas pedal.

"You got it. Go a little faster," I hedge. The car jolts forward and then back as she sucks in a breath, taking her foot off of the gas completely. "Hey, it's okay." I place my hands over hers. "Just a little softer this time." I lead her back into her own lane, because she was drifting over the white line. "You focus on the pedals, and I'll help with the wheel, okay?"

"Okay." She nods.

The dark, closed businesses pass by slowly as the speedometer climbs slowly. "There you go, you got it. Are you ready to take the wheel back?"

"Yeah," she sounds confident, like herself.

Slowly, I let go of the wheel and rest my hands on her waist. Her back is rod straight, her head almost brushing the roof of the car since she's sitting on my lap.

She drives a little close to the center line, but it's dead out and a four lane, so I'm not too worried.

"You're doing great, Reyna." I lean forward and kiss the leather of my cut. It hasn't slipped my attention that she hasn't taken it off. Her turn is a bit jerky, but soon we're leaving town behind and venturing onto the dark highway. She naturally speeds up, this time a lot smoother, and she handles the wheel like a pro. "You don't need me anymore. I'll give you directions and you can drive us home."

"Okay," she says quietly.

Reyna presses the brake, and I push the gearshift into park in my driveway. The cabin of the car is thick with tension.

"Lucid Dreams" by Juice WRLD plays softly through the car speakers.

"Leo," she sighs, leaning forward against the wheel.

"Do you want me, Siren?" I ask, closing the gap between us and pressing my chest to her back. "Do you want me as much as I want you?"

"Yes," she whispers almost inaudibly.

"You can't wait, can you?" I tease her.

"No." she shakes her head. *Me fucking either.*

I tap her hip. "Lift up." Her manicured hands grip the steering wheel, and she lifts her ass off of me. When she does that, I slide down her sweatpants and panties and I unbutton and unzip my pants and free my cock.

With my hand wrapped around my dick, I use the other hand to guide her back and down onto it.

She moans as I slide into her and drops her head forward. How cliche is it to say that she feels like she was made for me? But she does. She's a perfect fit for me. Perfectly tight and warm. She's the best pussy I've ever had, and she doesn't even have to do anything. But it's more than that. I feel *more* when I'm with her.

Reyna rides me, holding onto the steering wheel to bounce up and down.

She just started and I already feel myself wanting to come; how embarrassing. "Slow down, Siren," I say, but she ignores me, continuing at a pace that she obviously likes. Her moans grow louder and shorter, and I feel her pussy flutter around my cock. She's about to come.

I have to make sure she's first. I suck my index finger into my mouth and reach around her body and place it right on her clit, rubbing it furiously to match her pace.

Her breath stutters as she sucks it in, and then I feel the

strong convulsions of my pussy walls. She lets out a long moan, and a gentleman would let her calm down before he fucked her into eternity and came himself, but I'm not a gentleman.

I move my hands to her ass and lift her up and hold her while I pound up into her. Her pussy contracts harder, and Reyna screams, almost sounding like she's crying. Hell, she might be, but I'm not stopping.

"No one else, Siren. You got that?" I grunt, about to bust my load. She answers me with a moan, and I let loose, exploding inside of her.

I didn't specify that I meant *I* didn't want anyone, but I'll let her figure that out.

I drop my ass to my seat and pull Reyna's panties and sweats back up. She settles into my lap again, her breaths huffing out quickly, making the foggy windows worse.

"I'd invite you to stay the night in my room, but I plan on finishing the bathroom tomorrow and I don't want to wake you with it," I say, my heart slowly calming down.

"You don't have to lie. I'm a big girl and am fine staying in my own room." Reyna stays facing forward.

"I'm not lying." I lean forward, my hands gliding up her sides and wrapping around her. "I want you in my bed with me."

"You just want to fuck me again." Her attitude is back, but I wouldn't change that.

"Maybe," I agree. "But maybe I also just want to sleep next to you. Wake up to you in the morning."

She turns her head, her long hair sweeping across my stomach. "Then finish your bathroom and ask me again."

"I will," I promise.

She turns her body this time and leans close to me. "Goodnight, pet," she whispers against my lips.

My hand shoots up and wraps around her throat. Not tightly,

sort of. "What did I say about calling me that?" I ask, raising my brows.

"If you're not one of my clients, then prove it," she answers, undisturbed.

I smirk. *This bitch.* She's so manipulative. "Get out and take that sexy ass upstairs, then. You're in my bed from now on."

32

———

REYNA

MY SNEAKERS THUD AGAINST THE STAIRS AS I MAKE MY WAY UP, with Leo behind me. I really need to stop letting him come inside of me, since I'm not on my birth control anymore, but I like it. Feeling his cock thicken right before he's about to come almost gives me another orgasm.

The wood floors from downstairs continue upstairs into Leo's bedroom—shocker—but at least up here he has a soft shag rug under the bed. It could be a little cringy, but I don't mind it. I bet it will feel great on wintry mornings when getting out of bed.

Other than that, his room is quite plain. A king sized bed sits on the back wall with one nightstand on one side... and that's it.

Alright, if I'm staying up here, this has got to change. This entire house needs a makeover.

I stop myself and those kinds of thoughts. I'm not sure how much longer I'll be here.

"What are you thinking about, Siren?" Leo steps around me, fisting the back of his collar and pulling his shirt over his head.

Tan abs greet me and I lose my train of thought for a moment, which is embarrassing. I knew Leo was hot, and I knew he had to have an impressive body under his clothes, but thinking it and actually seeing it are two very different things, and this is *much* better.

"Uh," I stall while my brain reboots. "I've never slept with somebody before," I admit honestly. "Or I guess I have now since you stayed with me the night after that party, but other than that..." I trail off. Why am I saying all of this?

He tosses his shirt in a hamper by the door that I missed and starts undoing his jeans. "I didn't sleep the night you took the molly. I was too worried, so tonight will be the first night I share a bed with someone, too."

I roll my eyes, shifting on my feet. "There you go again, lying to me."

Leo cocks his head, dropping his jeans and stepping out of them. "When are you going to realize that I don't have to lie to you?" He walks towards me. "I've fucked a lot of women, and I couldn't tell you the names of at least half of them, but I've never shared a bed with anyone." He closes the gap between us and takes my chin between his finger and thumb. "You make me do shit I've never done before. *Feel* shit I've never felt before. I don't know how to do this, but I want to," he pauses, his hazel eyes flicking between mine. "With you."

"What do you mean, Leo? Are you asking me to be your girl-friend?" My brows rise. I didn't expect this. I didn't think he was feeling the way I was.

His brows pull together, and he shakes his head, letting go of my chin. "I don't know what we are, but I know that you're mine and I don't want to mess with anyone else, so I guess I'm yours."

"You guess?" I snap, placing my hands on my popped hip.

"I don't fucking know, Reyna. Do you know how to do this?" He spins around, stomping to the bed and sitting down heavily.

He seems really serious about this. "No, but I don't think this is how it's done."

Leo pushes off of the bed and storms to me. He roughly

grabs me by the hips and pulls me into his body, one of his hands threading into the hair at the back of my head. "You're mine and I'm yours, and we can figure the rest out as we go, okay?" He leans toward my face, only a breath away.

"What do you want from me?" I breathe, barely a whisper.

Leo's tongue runs over his plump bottom lip as if in slow motion. "I want to know who you are in the dark when no one's watching, when no one's there to soothe your needs." He blinks, his long, black lashes fanning over his cheeks.

"Okay," I finally agree.

Butterflies. Leo gives me butterflies. And those butterflies fill me with dread because I realize that I'm too far into this now to back out.

"Let's go to bed, Siren." Leo lets go of my head and hip and takes my hand, pulling me toward his bed.

33

REYNA

THUD, THUD, THUD! A HAMMERING NOISE ROUSES ME FROM SLEEP, and my head swivels as I look around the unfamiliar room. I forgot I fell asleep in Leo's bed last night. It's even more unimpressive in the daylight.

I briefly remember cuddling before I lost consciousness. But I'm not going to revisit that right now.

Thud, thud; there's the hammering again. It's coming from the ensuite. Wow. He was serious when he said he was finishing the bathroom today.

On soft feet, I cross the bedroom and peek inside the bathroom.

And I'm pleasantly surprised. White marble countertop with a large white basin, and deep navy painted cabinets. A white tile floor with a large glass shower and a giant freestanding tub sitting under a wide window that overlooks the pond. Leo is hanging the large mirror above the sink, his arms flexing as he lifts the heavy mirror onto the wall.

"This doesn't even look like it belongs in the cabin. It's the complete opposite of every other room." I admire the bright and airy bathroom.

"I wanted something different in here." Leo stays focused on the mirror, before placing a scale on top to make sure it's even.

"It's beautiful." My eyes scan the room. "You should add some light blue accessories in here. Like flowers or rugs or something."

Leo looks around the room, his eyes stopping on me. "That's a good idea. I'll do it."

"Are you done? I'm hungry." I change the subject when his gaze feels too heavy.

He quirks a brow and his hazel eyes fill with mischief. "Then go make something."

My jaw sets as I bite the inside of my lip. Someone is feeling bratty this morning. "Aren't you hungry too?"

Leo cocks his head, his smiling only growing. "No." Without another word, I turn on my heel and walk back into the bedroom. His cocky chuckle follows me into the room. "I know you know how to cook. I remember you cooking at the clubhouse."

I turn around to find him leaning against the doorframe, his shoulder pressed against it and his head cocked to the side. Smiling sarcastically, I spin and take the first step downstairs.

His laugh fills the loft style bedroom, spilling over the railing and into the rest of the house as his feet pound behind me and he catches up to me on the stairs. "Why do you have an attitude?"

"I don't know, Leo," I snap.

He steps around me and to the step below me, taking my hands in his. "Tell me what you want me to do," he soothes me... and I like it.

His words slip over me like water filling a room, gliding over my edges and softening them. "I don't know how to cook." I lick my lips, staring into his hazel eyes, even though the vulnerability in my voice makes me want to vomit.

His thick, brown brows pull together. "But you made your-self breakfast at the clubhouse."

I shake my head, letting the warmth of his fingers infiltrate my body and alter my being. I'm slowly letting myself rely on Leo. To depend on him. "That's all I can make."

"Okay." He nods sharply. "Then I'll teach you how to make more things." He drops one of my hands and leads me down the steps with the other. "You don't have to fight with me, Siren. Just tell me what you need and I'll make it happen."

By the time we're finally done and sitting down to eat, we have an entire breakfast buffet. Leo taught me how to make breakfast burritos, omelets, bacon, sausage patties, and pancakes. It was all fairly easy, and I could have figured it out on my own, but it was nice to be taught.

I grab a little of everything. I'm excited to try everything that we made together.

Leo chuckles as he sets down a glass of orange juice in front of me. "What?" I ask, pouring syrup over my pancake.

"It's sweet to see you excited about something. I don't think I've ever seen it before." He sits down next to me at the kitchen peninsula and takes the syrup after I set it down.

"I'm proud of what we made."

Leo takes a bite, chewing slowly as we let silence fill the room. "Living here with me is a lot different from when you lived at La Lujuria; do you miss it?"

Shaking my head, I swallow my bite of sausage. "No."

"But here you don't have maids or chefs, and you have to be making less money at Second," he argues.

There is no doubt in my mind that this life is better than the one I had. I turn to look at Leo. "I didn't have friends at La Lujuria. I didn't have you."

We finish our meal in silence, and as Leo is taking our plates to the sink, he stops and turns back to me. "I know you said you used to go to Seattle, but have you traveled anywhere else?"

"No," I answer, and when he purses his lips out of what I can only assume is pity, I turn my gaze to the counter and wipe up nonexistent crumbs with my napkin. "A client once asked me to go to the Maldives with them, but the club turned him down because they didn't want me leaving the island."

Plates being set on the counter in the corner of my vision pulls my attention up to Leo. "Well, since I obviously can't trust you here by yourself, do you want to come with me on the next club trip? It's to California." His smile makes it clear that he's teasing me for Huntley and I being arrested, and I nod, a small smile pulling at my lips.

"Yeah, that sounds fun."

"Okay, now go move all of your stuff upstairs to my room and clean out your stuff from the downstairs bathroom because I'm going to redo that room soon." He picks up the plates and takes them to the sink to rinse before putting them in the dishwasher.

I swipe my phone from the counter and turn to do exactly as Leo said when my phone vibrates in my hand.

UNKNOWN:

I'm getting restless, little whore.

34

LEO

My Mustang rolls through the gates of the clubhouse, and I pull as close to the front door as possible.

Reyna looks between me and the door, the crockpot sitting in her lap. "You do know I won't melt in the rain, right?"

"Uhh..." I stammer. "I was trying to be gentlemanly," I snap.

Her dark brows pull together and the corner of her top lip lifts. "Don't." She opens the car door and gets out with the crockpot of chorizo queso.

Today feels like a sorority rush. Cale, Saint, and Finn have invited a few guys that want to prospect for the club to come for a club dinner. They said it would be a good way to get to know them. We'll have some drinks and food, and get to know them better than at a party. Mason, Jack, and I sat this one out, still ashamed of the last prospect we brought in. Obviously we can't pick them, so we didn't even try.

But the club is dangerously low on members, and with the shit we inevitably find ourselves in, we could lose everyone and the Washington chapter would be extinct.

So sorority welcome party it is.

Luckily, we're not begging for prospects—the numbers for new guys aren't even close to being low—so we're not desperate.

Unfamiliar cars have already filled the parking lot, and I hurry inside, splashing through the puddles with my sneakers.

Reyna's around the back of the bar, leaning over the top to grab the electrical cord. Her perky tits push up even higher when pressed against the bar top, and I groan loudly.

A few prospective members try to talk to me, offer their hands in greeting, but I push past them without speaking and beeline for the bar. A few guys are already taking an interest in Reyna, and that's not fucking happening. Not ever.

She straightens her back and plugs in the crockpot behind the bar. When I reach her, I take her chin in between my fingers and pull her face to mine. She's not even surprised, not stiff with shock. She molds into my body, fitting against me like she was made for me—with skin as soft as silk.

Her lips part for me and I make my claim on her clear as day for everyone to see. My free hand wraps around to her back and slides down to her jean clad ass. I squeeze her cheek and press her into me harder, causing a small moan to pour into my mouth from hers.

"Get a room," Huntley teases, and I pull my mouth away from Reyna's.

Taking a step back—a small one—I slide my cut down my arms and place it over Reyna's. "Wear this," I demand, my eyes falling down her skintight, low cut, black, long sleeve top and jeans.

"Again?" she slightly whines.

"I want everyone in here to know that you're mine." My voice stays stern and I wait for her to slide her arms into my cut.

With a roll of her eyes, she does.

Satisfied, I turn and leave the bar. Huntley grins like a maniac at the front of the bar, and I catch Saint's eye from across the room as he shakes his head and turns back to one of the new guys.

I grab a water from one of the huge drink barrels when Jack grabs hold of my arm. "We need to talk." His blonde hair hangs in his eyes. Of course, he's not mingling.

When I nod, he releases me and walks away without turning to make sure I'll follow—he knows I will. I wonder if he's finally going to fill me in on that girl in California.

I follow Jack into the chapel, and he closes the door behind me. Oh, he is! I've never seen him with a girl, so this is exciting. Finally, he'll get some pussy. Maybe that's what he needs, something to loosen his death grip on his composure. It'd be so great to see him let loose just once. He's too controlled, too serious— but I bet if you asked him about me, he'd say the opposite of me. I never think of the consequences, only living to have a good time.

We're too different to be friends, but maybe that's what makes us the best friends. I've never had someone go so hard for me. Never had someone be so in tune with me, even if we're so different in every other way.

Jack clears his throat and fishes around in his pocket, pulling out a dainty tennis necklace. "I got this for Reyna." He holds it out to me.

"Uhhh..." I take it from him, very fucking confused. This is not where I thought this conversation was going to go.

He scoffs, his face turning into a sneer. "Not like that, idiot. It's for you to give to her; it has a tracking device in it."

"Jack," I sigh.

He shakes his head, his features hardening. "I don't trust her, Leo."

"She doesn't go anywhere without me," I argue softly. I don't see what Jack does. I don't see his concern.

"After the year we've had, it's better to be safe than sorry." He crosses his toned arms across this chest.

"Fine," I relent. She'll think I'm getting her a nice gift, and Jack will shut the fuck up. We all win. Well, kinda. Reyna's still being tracked without her knowledge, but whatever.

Turning the knob, I push through the door and walk back into the main room of the clubhouse. The queen and princess of the Outlaws sit at a high top table, with Cale standing behind Reese and rubbing her shoulders.

And of course Reyna and Huntley are standing by the pool table whispering together with evil little smiles. The two of them together is such a horrible idea, but the best thing that could happen at the same time. Huntley is the definition of 'ride or die' and that's exactly what Reyna needs. And I think Reyna is exactly the kind of friend that Huntley needs as well. Huntley likes to nurture people. It's why she enjoys working at the shop. She likes to be there for people, to listen to them, and to help them. She likes to help the young guys that work for Finn; to teach them how to manage their finances, and how to survive in life. The guys come in and vent to Huntley. They ask her if their interest rate is good when they go to buy a car and how much they should put down for a house. Reyna needs that. Not financial advice, just someone to listen to her without any judgments, because I'm sure that woman has seen some shit that she'll eventually need to unload.

"Hey." Mason's hand cups my shoulder, stopping me. "Did Jack give you the necklace?" he says slightly under his breath.

"Oh, was that your fucking idea?" I snap, annoyed.

"No." Mason shakes his head, pulling me closer to the wall and further away from the crowd of people. "It was Jack's. I just installed the tracker and I'm the one who has the program, but when you're ready for it, I'll give you the login."

I roll my eyes and pull my arm from his light grip. "Whatever, you guys will see that this was unnecessary."

"I'm sorry," Mason says, but I've already turned my back on him and started walking away. But I guess there's a small part of me who is still unsure about Reyna too, because I didn't give Jack the necklace back and tell him to shove it up his ass; so can I really be mad at them?

And I feel like such a dick for doubting her, but what if? The necklace doesn't have to be about mistrust. It could be for safety. We can never be too safe in our line of work, right? No, I'm still a dick.

Ah, fuck. I'd better get some food and get to know some of these new guys; some of them might be Outlaws soon.

———

OKAY, so these guys are pretty cool. A lot of them are clients of Saint's or Finn's, and a few of them work for Finn. They seem like good guys, but we'll know for sure after Mase runs *extensive* backgrounds on them. We're not skimping on that part like we did with fucking Archer. Fucking rat bastard. There's even a huge fucker that could rival Finn. I'd pay to get the two of them in the boxing ring, but Huntley would probably jump in with a fucking knife when she thought it went too far.

Things are winding down, and I'm happy we did a potluck-type dinner rather than a party like we used to. The mood was relaxed, and it was easy to listen to these guys and get to know them without the distraction of women, alcohol, and drugs; and it makes sure that they're joining for the right reasons.

Now, they'll enter the hang around phase, which we agreed as a club will be a lot longer than Archer's hang around time was, but we were desperate at the time, and we suffered because of it.

Man, fuck that guy. I'm still pissed off that he lied to us and was an undercover agent.

"You're not still mad at me, are you?" Jack asks, coming up next to me.

I level him with a glare from the corner of my eyes. "No," I sigh, my eyes shifting forward to find Reyna in the dwindling crowd.

"You're my brother, Leo, and not just my club brother. I will protect you at any cost, and I don't fucking trust her." I can't be mad at him. Jack is the most important person in my life.

"Why?" I almost plead. I can't understand where he's coming from.

Jack shakes his head, his lips slipping between his teeth as he glances at the floor. "I don't know exactly. It's just something in her eyes. They betray her."

"You're speaking in riddles." I roll my eyes.

His brown eyes slowly rise to mine. "I'm not trying to; I see it in her eyes."

Jack's officially lost the fucking plot. I have no idea what he's talking about anymore. "Does this have anything to do with that girl in California?"

Something passes through his eyes, but I can't make out what. "This has nothing to do with Sam."

"Who is she?" I ask, frustrated. I'm tired of my love life being the only one up for judgment.

"I already told you." I can see the storm doors slam closed behind his eyes, and I back off. The last thing I want to do is push him to the point that it hurts our relationship.

"When you're ready to talk about her, I'm here," I offer.

He shakes his head, his lips pursed. "There's nothing to talk about."

"Alright." I glance around the clubhouse. All the new guys are gone, as well as Cale and Reese. Saint, Allie, and Mason are gathering up their things and Reyna's watching us from a table while talking to Huntley and Finn. "I'm gonna head home, you alright here?"

"Been doing alright." His jaw clenches.

Biting my lip, I feel terrible. I've been so engrossed in Reyna that I've forgotten my brother is here by himself. "I don't like that you've been here alone."

"Don't worry about me, I like it." His jaw relaxes, and some warmth seeps back into his eyes.

"You know you always have a place with me, right?" I ask, guilt flooding in.

He nods. "I know. Now get the fuck out, I'm tired." He pushes my chest and I fall back a step, laughing at the small smile that appears on his face.

"Alright, I'll see you later, brother." I pull Jack into a quick hug, the only kind he'll let me give him, and go get the crockpot so Reyna and I can go home.

35

REYNA

Tonight was boring. All I did was talk to Huntley and let Leo grope me when his masculinity was threatened—which honestly wasn't that bad. It was sexy to see him jealous. But I'm still bored. These club events are dull and all we ever do is sit around and talk. Where's the excitement, the thrill? I mean, come on, this damn clubhouse has a strip club, for fuck's sake. Why are we just sitting around having dinner with new guys?

"Why are you pouting?" Leo asks, holding the giant crockpot. My life went from personal chefs and Cartier bracelets to potlucks and MC clubhouses. The worst part is that I'm not upset about that. What has Leo done to me?

"I'm bored. You brought me out of the house just for this?" My eyes sweep over the empty clubhouse.

"I'm sorry this wasn't a college house party with molly," he sasses me, setting the crockpot on a nearby table. "Was there something else you had in mind for tonight?"

My eyes fall on the double doors at the back of the room. "Do you want to see my routine for tomorrow night?"

Leo chuckles. "You don't get enough of stripping every weekend. You want to do it on your time off, too?"

I shrug. "I enjoy dancing."

"Fine." Leo gestures towards the private dance room and I take the lead, walking toward it.

I wandered inside when I was here alone one time. I looked through every room in the clubhouse. It was underwhelming and needs an update. That includes the back room with mirrors as walls and a couple of stages with poles. A plaque above the door calls it Purgatory. Purgatory looks like a cheap strip club with sticky floors and spotty mirrors in the bathroom.

The room is pitch black when I push one door open, but it soon illuminates into a deep red when Leo flips on the light behind me. The door clicks closed and Leo flicks the lock.

I watch Leo in the mirror in front of me. He saunters up to me, his arm brushing against my shoulder as he passes.

I turn to look up at him. "The sound system is by the door." He looks down at me before walking toward a chair in front of the center stage.

I hook my phone up to the large sound system, selecting "Under The Influence" by Chris Brown, and then I unbuckle my jeans, sliding them down my legs and kicking them off along with my heels. Dropping Leo's cut, I pull my shirt over my head and drop them in a pile unceremoniously, leaving me in my bra and thong. I hadn't planned on dancing when I got dressed this evening. In any case, it doesn't matter. What's important is what's underneath, anyway.

Hitting play on the song, I walk toward Leo, swaying my hips. He sits facing forward, but turns his head to watch me, his jaw jutting out in a sharp line, the red LEDs reflecting off of it.

"Don't do that." I shake my head, placing my hands on his shoulders and straddling his waist.

"Do what?" he asks lazily, his gaze dipping to my breasts as his hands cup my ass, then slide down my thighs and back up.

My skin ignites where he touches me, his fingertips leaving behind a tingle as he rubs up and down my thighs. I drop my forehead to his shoulder, resting it there while I revel in his warm touches. "Fall in love with me." I turn my head and say into his neck.

"I should spank your ass for leaving my cut on the floor." One of his powerful hands glides up my back and pulls me away from him by the back of my neck. There isn't a trace of playfulness in his hazel eyes as he stares up at me.

I sway my hips, my pussy sliding over his half erection. "Pity for you, I'd like that."

"Do you want me to spank you?" His dark brows rise, and he rests his head against the back of the chair.

"Maybe." I place my hands on his knees and lean backward, sticking my chest out as I ride him.

"Then I won't reward you with it." One side of his mouth tips into a smirk, and I say nothing more. I don't *know* what more to say. I didn't expect to feel this way about him.

Instead, I do the worst possible thing. Leaning forward, I grasp his face in my hands and guide him to my mouth. I don't want to think anymore, I just want to feel him. I want to feel our bodies in sync with one another. I want to feel his heartbeat, and forget about all the pressures that are placed upon us. I just want to exist in a world with only the two of us, where I wasn't an escort running for my life and he wasn't a member of the motorcycle club I had to step on.

Pulling away, tears threaten to spill over, and I push off Leo. I turn around, but big hands grab me by the hips and pull me to sit on his lap.

"I don't need to see any more, this is already too inappropriate for anyone but me to see." His hand wraps around my neck and he pulls me backward to rest against his chest.

His warmth bleeds into me, soothing my soul and making

my heart clench. Why did I let myself fall for him? I know this is all going to end soon. It has to.

Leo's palm slides around my stomach and angles down, slipping into my thong. Two fingers spread me open and his middle finger rubs over my clit.

With a sigh, I drop my head onto his shoulder, closing my eyes. Leo's lips brush over my ear, and his breath fans over it as he whispers, "Are you hiding anything from me, Siren?"

My heart beats faster, and I can't be sure of the exact reason, or maybe it's a mixture. "Of course I have things I've never told you, just as you've never told me everything." My hips lift involuntarily, trying to press harder against his light touches.

"I'm an open book. You can ask me anything and I'll tell you." His hand squeezes the sides of my neck, leaving my breathe way open, but still causing my head to float. "What would you do if I betrayed you?"

His hand tightens, this time cutting off my breathing, and his other hand cups my pussy. "Why would you say that?" he snaps, and I watch his jaw clench from the corner of my eyes.

After a beat, he loosens his grip enough for me to talk. "It was just a hypothetical." My brows dip, glaring at him.

"If you cheated on me, I'd kill whoever you slept with. If you betrayed my club, I'd kill you." I swallow roughly against his hand, staring into his stone eyes. "Does that answer your hypothetical?" I minutely nod my head once and he lets go of my throat. "Don't ask stupid questions, Siren."

Every time I get a glimpse of the biker Leo, it terrifies me. But it also makes a small part of me feel safe.

A rush of cold air sweeps over my pussy as Leo pulls his warm hand away, and he lets go of my neck as well. I turn around to look at him, wondering why he stopped.

He jostles me around, reaching into his back pocket for something, and holds his fisted palm between us. "I got you something." He slowly opens his hand to reveal a beautiful tennis necklace, the LEDs glinting off of the row of diamonds.

"Why?" I ask, taking the necklace to admire. It's beautiful.

He continues to stare at the necklace in my hands as he speaks. "No woman has ever meant as much to me as you do."

"Thank you." I raise it to my neck and turn around, indicating for him to fasten it on me. "But you know what would be even better," I say as his strong fingers brush against the back of my neck and hook the necklace. "If you would fuck me in it." I turn back to face him with a smirk.

"How can I ever deny you, Siren?" he says, his warm eyes turning lustful in a half-lid gaze. "You can thank me with my cock in your mouth." His tongue darts out to wet his plump lips.

I slide out of his lap and onto my knees on the floor. I hold his eyes as I widen his legs and move between them, reaching for the button of his jeans.

Pulling his jeans down his legs, I reach behind me and unhook my bra, tossing it to the side and leaning down and running my tongue up the bottom of Leo's shaft. I slide my tongue side to side as I slowly work my way up. Leo grunts as I reach the sensitive spot under his tip, his head dropping back onto the chair while he widens his legs further.

I lightly suck on his thick head as I fondle his balls, rolling them from one side of my palm to the other.

I want to worship Leo's cock and the pleasure he gives me. Having sex for myself is a whole other experience than when I'm paid to do it. No one will ever compare to Leo.

With a firm grip, I work the rest of Leo's dick while I suck harder on the head, adding a twist to my wrist.

Leo's hand slides over my face, from my cheeks and back through my hair, collecting it and piling it on the back of my head where he holds it out of the way for me. Which is sweet until he uses that to push me further down his cock.

But I don't reprimand him, I just remove my hand and relax my throat, and take him into my mouth, soaking his dick in my saliva and bathing in the pride that his sigh causes. Maybe it's my love of performing, but I love blowing a person's mind, leaving them thoughtless and trying to catch their breath.

I release Leo's dick with a pop and move forward, pressing his cock between my tits. His eyes are glued to my chest as I bounce up and down.

"You have the most beautiful fucking tits." He stares, his mouth falling open with a sigh.

"What's better?" I ask, letting saliva drip out of my mouth and onto the head of his dick. "My pussy, my mouth, or my tits?"

"I thought we already talked about stupid questions, Siren. I might take your ass tonight to add that to the list." He grabs my shoulders and pulls me to stand.

Leo skillfully pulls his legs out of his jeans and pulls his shirt over his head, tossing it onto the floor. His muscular hands turn me around and walk me to the stage where he guides me into a kneeling position on top of.

Standing behind me, he pulls my panties down my legs and pushes between my shoulder blades until my face rests against the cold stage. I should be concerned about whatever bacteria is on this stage and getting on my face, but that's the last thought on my mind right now.

"This pussy is my home and I'll always come back to it." He licks from my clit to my opening. "I promise to never stray from it." He repeats the motion.

"Leo," I moan, arching my back to give him better access.

He fucks my pussy with his tongue as his finger strokes over my clit.

I groan. More. I need more. But before I can voice that, Leo pulls away from me and rubs his cock through the sloppy mess of my pussy. "I really need to quit fucking you raw, but I'm too obsessed with how you feel wrapped around me. I can't stop."

I feel like a toy wound too tight, I just need to release some pressure—oh *fuck!*

Leo pushes into me in one long, fluid motion, his balls lightly tapping against my clit and making me clench around him.

I agree with him; I love the feeling when he fucks me without a condom; I love to feel the ridge of his head as is slides against me. I really should tell him we need to stop, though. I'm not on birth control.

Next time. I'll tell him next time. *If there is a next time.*

Leo's big hands grip my hips tightly as he thrusts into me, waving his hips and making my eyes roll into the back of my head. He knows how to hit every spot inside of me to make me light up.

"I love this tight pussy," he grunts, his hips picking up speed. He bends over me, shifting just enough inside of me that he sets me off. "Suck," he demands, his thumb pressing against my mouth.

I take his thumb in my mouth and suck, but as he fucks me harder, my orgasm crests, and I bite down on his thumb as the waves crash over me. I can't help it, I lose all function of my body, becoming a slave to the sensations as he fucks me through the orgasm.

"Fuck," Leo hisses as he pulls his thumb from my mouth when I finally release it. He pulls out of me, pushing on one side of my hip to get me to roll over.

Listlessly, I follow his demand and land on my back, not even the bite of the cool stage floor breaking through my post orgasm haze.

Leo opens my legs wide and holds them at the ankles, pushing back inside of me.

I watch his abs flex as he fucks me hard, a bead of sweat running between the valleys of his abs. His hands squeeze my ankles so tightly, I'm sure they'll leave bruises, and his eyes screw shut as his mouth hangs open in a permanent sigh.

"Look at me, Leo!" I snap. His eyes open halfway, his lids drooping lazily as he stares down at me. His chest rises and falls rapidly as he pumps into me quicker. "Who are you fucking?" I ask.

"I'm fucking what's mine," he growls.

I can tell he's close. The pained look on his face is a dead giveaway, so I reach down and circle my clit with my finger, trying to match his pace.

His eyes fall to watch my fingers and he thrusts a few more times before he quickly pulls out and fists his cock, pumping it until hot ropes of cum land on my stomach.

That sight pushes me over the edge and just as I'm about to come, Leo shoves three fingers inside of me and fingers me quickly, my pussy choking his fingers in my orgasm.

"Sorry, baby, I couldn't hold it off any longer." Leo dips his head, pulling his fingers out of my pussy and sucking them into his mouth.

I watch him hungrily as aftershocks ripple through my body.

Leo lays down next to me, propped on his elbow and his finger dips into the cum sprinkled across my stomach.

His brown hair hangs in his eyes, a few strands stuck to his forehead with sweat and his sharp jaw and cheek bones pop and he stares intently at the mess he made.

Leo's finger moves here and there, and I pay it no mind as I stare up at him. In my mind, I can see a sand timer quickly losing its sand. Our time is almost up. We'll have to return to the real world soon.

Finally, Leo sits up and stands, hopping off the stage and grabbing his jeans. I prop myself up on my elbows and look down at my stomach. It's not perfect. Milky white letters trail off into nothing or just clear liquid, but it's still clear enough to tell what he wrote. *Mine.*

After buttoning his jeans, Leo steps onto the stage with his shirt in his hand. He kneels beside me, looking into my eyes as he wipes the cum from my stomach. His intent is clear. He has marked me in his own fucked up way.

Leo drops the shirt beside us and runs his finger under the crease of my breasts and over my sternum. "This is where I want you to get my tattoo."

"What?" I snap, raising my head.

"Whenever you're ready. I want everyone to see a permanent reminder that you're mine, unless you'd rather go out covered in my cum every day." He smiles, but I have a hard time believing he's joking.

"You're insane." I shoo him away and sit up. And I'm in the boat right next to him because now I'm thinking up designs.

Being his has been the only thing I've ever been proud of being.

36

LEO

THE RENOVATIONS FOR THE LIQUOR STORE ARE PROGRESSING A LOT slower than Jack and I hoped, but we're almost there. Dropping my neck from side to side, I let out a sigh when it cracks loudly; staring at a piece of paper, doing boring shit has never been my favorite thing. My best memory is graduating from high school and never having to do homework again. Until now.

Filling out this alcohol permit feels a lot like homework: answering questions and providing documents. I'm stuck in the office at Second, the music making the walls thump, and I check my phone for the time. Reyna should be going up soon, so I'll take a break from this to head out to watch her.

Knock, knock. Someone thumps on the closed door.

"Come in," I call, staying seated at the desk.

The door pops open and Stephanie, the house mom, slips her head inside, her brown hair falling over her shoulder in a curtain. "I just wanted to let you know Lyla is going to go up for Reyna tonight."

I turn my body toward her, my entire attention on her. "What's wrong with Reyna?"

She shakes her head, dismissing my concerns. "She just

doesn't feel well. She's showering now and then I think she's going to come talk to you."

Stephanie is old enough to be my mom, and she takes great care of the girls here, so I trust Reyna is in fine hands while here. "Okay, let her know I'm waiting to take her home."

She nods, a warm smile on her face. "Will do, hun."

The door closes again and I try to focus on the application again, but I can't. It couldn't be something she ate, right? I feel fine and we eat the same meals. Maybe she caught something from a customer or another stripper. I should go check on her.

I'm pushing the chair backward when the office door opens again. Mason steps inside, closing the door behind him.

"Hey, brother, what's up?" I pile the form together on my desk and head for the door. It's odd that Mason is here. He definitely wouldn't be here without Allie, and this doesn't really seem like her kind of place.

"I'm here to talk to you." He crosses his arms across his chest, the hood of his black hoodie framing his eyes.

"Can it wait?" I reach for the doorknob.

"No." Mason shakes his head.

Sighing, I run my hand through my hair, noticing he has his laptop with him. Must be some hacker shit he dug up.

I nod once and go back to my chair, and Mason follows me around the back of the desk, setting his laptop down once I'm seated.

"I got Reyna's DNA results back." He opens his laptop and I see a missing child notice.

Even as a toddler, I recognize her guarded blue eyes.

"Abigail Stenson," I read off the name. "This is Reyna?" I ask, even though I know it is.

"Yeah." Mase nods. "Her uncle did some time and her family's DNA was in the police database from the crime scene."

My head snaps up to Mason. "Crime scene?" I ask, my heart beating out of my chest.

"Her family was murdered. Mom, dad, older brother. Not too long after, her uncle died in a prison fight. They never found Abigail."

"Who did it? Who took her?" I ask, my head spinning. I had kind of expected something like this, but I hadn't prepared myself for it to be a reality.

Mase sighs and bends over, clicking a few things on his laptop and pulling up a list of names. "The Tacoma police thought Los Lobos had something to do with it. They interrogated several of the members at the time, but they couldn't make anything stick. Witness went missing and the main believer that it was Los Lobos was murdered in prison."

"Reyna's uncle?" I ask, though I already know that's the answer.

He nods. "Yup. The case went cold, but Abigail is still considered a missing person."

"Does she have any family left?" I turn the chair so I'm facing Mason.

"No." He shakes his head. "Maybe some distant cousins, but none that she would have ever met."

I sigh heavily, closing his laptop and sliding it toward him. I don't need to see anything else. Test results, police files—none of that sounds fun to sift through.

"Are you going to tell her?" Mason grabs his laptop.

My head hits the back of the chair as I lean back. "Am I going to tell her that the gang who raised her are most likely the same gang that murdered her entire family and then they trafficked and groomed her?" *Fuck, that sounds worse out loud than it did in my head.* I drag my hand down my face. "I don't know. I need some time to figure out how."

"Well, let me know if you want copies of everything I found. I gotta get out of here before Allie loses her shit though, so I'll see you later, alright?" Mason backs away from me but stops and smiles, pulling his phone out of his pocket. "I'm leaving now," he answers his phone. "Yeah, I'm with Leo and Jack's somewhere around here." He watches me as he listens to whoever's on the phone, most likely Allie or Saint. "Okay, I'll let them know," he pauses, listening again. "Yeah, place the order and I'll pick it up on the way home." He says a goodbye, clearly for Saint and *not* Allie, and hangs up.

"What's up?" I ask.

He slips his phone into his pocket. "We have to make another run to California."

"Is something wrong?" My palms sweat as I prepare myself for the worst.

"No." Mase shakes his head. "The California chapter just has another buyer, so they need ammo."

My body relaxes against the chair again. "When do we leave?"

"Saints working that out now, but the entire club isn't going." Mason adjusts the hood on his head with one hand, his other still holding his laptop.

"Who's not going?" My eyes narrow. It's a little odd, but I guess it's not that big of a deal. The whole club doesn't *have* to go.

Mason chews on the inside of his lip. "Me and Cale, and I think Saint's trying to convince Finn to stay too, but we know he won't."

"It's probably best for Cale to stay with Reese right now," I say. The fact that the single guys—me and jack—and Saint, the president, are the ones going, hasn't slipped past me though. Sometimes I miss when everyone was single. The clubhouse was more lively with everyone spending their free time there. I love Reese, Huntley, and Allie as if they were my sisters, but sometimes I miss my brothers.

A soft knock interrupts us, the door pushing open, and Reyna peeks in. Mason and I look at her and then at each other before I speak, breaking the tense silence. "I have to take Reyna home, so we'll talk later, okay?"

"Yeah." Mason nods. "I'm sure we'll have church soon, so I'll see you then, brother."

I stand to hug Mason before he leaves, and Reyna slips into the room, taking a seat on the opposite side of the desk.

Closing the door behind Mason, I turn around and walk to Reyna, kneeling before her. "You okay?" I ask, and as much as I try not to, I can't help but picture that missing child poster in my mind. I need to tell her, but probably not when she's sick.

"Yeah." Her nose scrunches as she screws her eyes shut. "Stephanie said it's a migraine. My head hurts and I feel nauseous."

"Okay, let's go home then. I'll stop by the pharmacy on the way and find you something for your head." Reyna nods, and I offer her my hand to stand.

Her delicate palm is clammy and weak in mine, so I keep hold of it the entire way to the car, and then all the way to the pharmacy, and then the whole way home.

37

REYNA

Leo's skin is warm under my cheek, and I slowly open my eyes. His sharp jaw juts toward the ceiling as he rests his head against the pillows, with his fingers still tangled in my hair from when he was massaging my head last night. It hurt more when I laid down flat, so Leo piled all the pillows behind him and I laid on him. I thought he would have moved me after I fell asleep, but he slept sitting up so that I could recline against his chest.

I don't even know what came over me. It started with a small headache, but it slowly set in to such intense pain that it hurt to open my eyes or think. I was in so much pain that I was nauseous. I've never had a migraine before, but it was a bitch.

The effects are still lingering, my head still aches a bit, and my stomach is in knots; I'm so hungry.

Leo's chest rises and falls steadily, one of his big hands resting against my hip. He taught me how to make pancakes, so I could make those for us, since he does so much for me all the time.

As gently as I can, I lift myself off of Leo, his fingers dragging through my hair as I pull away. He doesn't even stir as I crawl off of the bed. His neck is going to be so tense when he wakes up.

Downstairs, I mix the pancake batter in a large bowl and add fresh blueberries before spooning some onto the pan to make the pancakes.

As I watch the pancakes closely, waiting for the bubbles to pop so I can flip them, my mind wanders. I wonder if I could convince Leo to run away with me, start over in New York or Paris? No, he wouldn't leave his club members or his mom. Maybe I could disappear for a while, let things die out and then I could come back? But then I would lose everything I've worked for. I shouldn't have let myself fall for Leo, but how could I not? He talked to me about my fears and experiences, taught me to do things that I never had the opportunity to learn, things I wanted to learn. Leo sacrificed his comfort last night and massaged my head until I fell asleep; he takes better care of me than I do.

The plates thunk as I set them on the counter and dole pancakes onto each. The smell of salty butter mixed with the sweet scent of the blueberries hits my nose and my stomach turns all over again.

Shoving my plate aside, I drizzle maple syrup over Leo's pancakes and grab a fork.

Sunlight streams through the large windows, bathing the wood in a warm hue. Leo's husky voice, thick with sleep, drifts down the steps to me, and I stop tiptoeing up the stairs since he is obviously awake.

"Yeah, sounds good. We'll be ready." Leo's arm bulges while he holds the phone to his ear, the sunlight glowing against his skin.

His heavy-lidded eyes fall down my body and back up as he hangs up the phone and places it back on the side table.

"Who was that?" I ask, my toes sinking into the soft rug under the bed.

"Did you make me breakfast in bed?" Leo smirks, his white teeth shining in the light.

I roll my eyes and sit next to him, handing him the plate. "You massaged my head until you fell asleep last night. You're arguably more whipped than I am."

He takes a bite, shaking his head. "Nah, you cooked for me. You're one step away from begging me to put my babies in you."

"Ugh," I scoff. "Shut up and eat."

Loe laughs, picking up another bite. "Saint called. We're heading back to California in a few days."

"Oh." I purse my lips and shift my eyes to the bed, not sure if Leo was serious when he said I could go with them the next time they left.

He nudges me with his foot, commanding my eyes back to his. "That means you too."

"Oh," I repeat, this time smiling.

"It'll be fun." He pauses, letting himself chew and then swallow. "But it'll be chilly; we're taking the bikes."

"Okay." I nod and then stand. "I'll grab you some coffee and we can talk about the trip more."

"Thank you, baby." Leo's smile breaks my heart as I turn around and head down the stairs.

My hands shake as I unlock my phone and open the encrypted texting app.

REYNA:

We need to talk.

38

LEO

I'm fucking giddy; which is a feeling I never thought I would experience. But as I gather a change of clothes and pack my hygiene stuff, I can't stop smiling. Reyna is downstairs doing the same. We're only going to be gone one night again, so we don't need much, but I don't want her to be missing anything that she might want. I'd love to take trips with her on the bike, so I really want her to enjoy this small drive.

I hear her soft footsteps on the steps a moment before she walks into the bathroom. "What are we packing these in?" she asks, a stack of folded clothes in her arms.

"The saddlebags on the bike. I didn't want you to have to wear a backpack." I zip the toiletries bag closed.

"I don't mind," she answers quickly.

"Okay," I shrug, walking out of the bathroom to get my backpack from the closet. "We can pack our stuff in here then, but if it gets to be too much, we can stuff it in the saddlebags."

"It's a backpack, Leo." Reyna rolls her beautiful eyes, a small smile on her lips. She pretends that she's annoyed, and with anyone else, she probably would be. She's not used to someone taking care of her without expecting anything in return, so she's always taken care of herself. But I know she enjoys being able to let loose with me and let me take care of her. I know she loves that she can turn her brain off and let me make decisions for her. Not because she *can't* make them, but because she doesn't *want* to. And I'm honored that she would put that much trust in me to do that for her. I will never let her down.

I set the backpack on the bed and pack my change of clothes, then hold out my hand for hers.

Her bare feet pad across the wood floor and she offers me her slightly larger stack of clothes. I should have known she would pack more, but it's fine; I'd rent a uhaul for the trip if she wanted it.

After stuffing her clothes, I shove the toiletries bag on top and zip it closed. It's almost stuffed to the brim.

"Oh, I forgot something!" Reyna's eyes widen, and she reaches for the bag.

Snorting, I shake my head. "Okay, but remember, you're carrying that thing!" I call after her as she hurries down the steps with the bag.

I hear the dryer door open as I turn off the lights upstairs and make my way down to the main level.

Once my girl is done getting her shit from the dryer, we're meeting the guys and heading down to California. I can't wait for Reyna to see the different scenery. To see the palm trees and try some different food. This trip is going to be a lot more fun with her coming along.

I sit down on the couch to put my boots on when Reyna comes down the hallway. "Got everything?" I ask, glancing up at her as I'm bent over my legs. She nods, so I go back to lacing up my boots.

Reyna pulls the new leather jacket I bought her last night over a dark hoodie and watches as I slip my arms into my cut and place my handgun in the inner pocket.

"Are you planning for something to go wrong?" she asks, her brows creasing.

"I always plan for something to go wrong. That way I'm always prepared," I answer. I won't take any chances with her coming with us today; I will never let anything happen to her. My brothers taught me well. They protect their girls with a ferocity I've never seen before, and I plan to do the same.

Almost an hour later, Reyna and I pull to a stop in front of CM Roofing. Jack and Saint are already loading the van while Finn hunches over checking the pressure in his back tire.

I park to the side of him as Huntley comes out of the enormous warehouse, her helmet in her hands.

"Is Huntley coming too?" Reyna asks in my ear, holding my shoulders as she climbs off of my bike.

"I guess so." I shrug and hold her hand to stabilize her.

It makes sense that Finn would bring her along. Finn and Saint are expected to be here as the Prez and VP, but Saint can leave Allie at home with Mason.

I didn't tell Reyna what the run was for, just that we were taking stuff down to the California Chapter, and she didn't ask for details. Still now, she only watches as Jack and Saint stack the last few boxes and slam the back doors of the van closed. I'm not trying to keep things from her. If she asks, I'll tell her everything. But I believe it's probably best if she doesn't know what the club does. I don't want to put her in the position of ever having to be questioned.

Saint and Jack are taking the van since it only has two seats and Finn and I will lead on the bikes with our girls.

"Are you ready, Siren?" I ask, pulling Reyna toward me and wrapping her in my arms.

The sun is about to dip below the mountains and the van doors slam in the background, but all I see is the most beautiful woman in the entire universe bathed in the golden sunlight, her bottom lip caught between her teeth.

"Yeah." She nods. "Just a little nervous."

I kiss the small crease between her brows, smoothing it out. "There's no reason to be nervous, Reyna." My eyes fall down to the necklace I gave her. I run my finger along it, sucking my lips between my teeth before speaking again. "We're just going to visit some friends and come right back home."

THE SUN HAS LONG GONE DOWN, our headlights and the moon the only light along the long stretch of highway that we turned off on an hour ago. Finn and I ride side by side, and I lean forward, squinting. Our headlights fall on something blocking the road. Something large.

I turn to Finn and he shakes his head, confused. He holds up his left hand to let Jack know that we're slowing.

As we get closer, every hair on my body stands straight up. Something isn't right.

A large tractor trailer is blocking all lanes, but there isn't anyone in the cab, or anywhere around.

We all stop, our heads swinging from side to side, trying to find the driver of the truck.

Reyna presses against me and I reach down to hold her hand, to comfort both of us, but it's not there.

The cold muzzle of a gun digs under my chin and my breathing stops. "Turn off the ignition," Reyna says into my ear.

39

REYNA

The underside of Leo's chin pushes against the gun as he swallows, and it takes everything in me to keep my hand from shaking.

"This has to be a joke," he says, his voice harsh as he slowly moves his hand down to the tank and cuts the engine off.

My eyes track the men coming out from behind the trailer, guns pointed at the Outlaws. "I'm sorry," I whisper.

"Finn," Huntley's voice is sharp, only a hint of fear that would go unnoticed if you didn't know her.

"I know, Angel." His hard eyes bounce between the dozen men, no doubt weighing his options, but he doesn't have any, and he's realizing that.

"Engines off, toss the keys!" One man in a ski mask demands.

Finn's bike stops rumbling, as does the van behind us.

A thunderous clap echoes in the silence, as the grungy man with the dirty blonde hair steps from around the trailer last. The only clean part of his appearance is his leather cut.

"Fucking Colter. Can't say I'm happy to see you," Finn grunts.

Colter smirks, and his arrogance makes me nauseous. He's

so disgusting. "Smarter men would have been expecting me, but here you are," he gloats.

His boots crunch across the gravel, stopping beside us. He smiles down at me menacingly.

And offers me his hand.

"Don't fucking touch her," Leo growls, jostling the bike side to side as he lunges for Colter, who only laughs and backs away from Leo's swinging arm.

"Careful, little boy, she was my whore before she was yours." He smirks and offers me

his hand again.

Taking it, I step off of the bike, the cold of the night slapping me in the face.

"I'll kill you." Leo clenches his jaw, staring at Colter.

Colter drops his head back, laughing, and drops his gross arm over my shoulders. He straightens up, leveling Leo with a condescending look. "You'll be the ones dying tonight." He plucks the gun from my hand, shoving it in the back of his jeans.

With that one sentence, he steals the breath from my lungs, but I stay staring ahead, lacking the confidence to look at Leo.

"You fucking bitch," Huntley seethes from behind us a moment before I'm being pulled to the ground by my hair.

"Fuck, Huntley!" Finn roars as an ear piercing shot makes everyone stop.

Finn drags Huntley into his thick arms. Her eyes are wild and focused on me. Her shoes drag across the pavement as she fights against him.

With shaking hands, I smooth down my hair at the back of my head, staring at the ground. I didn't want her to be here. She wasn't supposed to be here.

Colter's pasty hand enters the corner of my vision, but I shoo it away. I don't want his help.

Pushing to my feet, I glance around the road. Men are

ushering Saint and Jack out of the van with guns pointed at them.

I caused this and I don't feel good about it in the least. As much as I don't want to, my eyes glance at Leo, and his glare spears me in place. So much hatred pours from his burning eyes, and it makes me hate myself.

Quickly, I look to the ground. I can't look at him anymore. I sold him and his club out to their biggest enemy. A man who wants them dead.

I spent the last two months spying on them, searching the clubhouse and Leo's cabin, and sending everything I could to Colter. I forged friendships to blend in easier, but along the way, they became less about a disguise and more because I enjoyed their company and they became dear to me. But yet here we are, because there was one thing that I wanted more than friendship.

Family.

"Tie them up," Colter gestures with a handgun. Men move at Colter's command, but he stops the guy heading for Leo. "You can tie up the hot headed one." He offers me the zip tie, and I can see in his eyes that this isn't a request.

I snatch the ties from his hand and walk behind Leo. I don't dare look at him, but I can feel his burning gaze on the side of my face. With as much strength as I can muster, which isn't much, I pull his arms behind his back and loop one tie around one of his wrists.

Colter turns around to watch Finn and Huntley, and Leo turns to the side to speak over his shoulder. "Why are you doing this?"

"Maybe this is who I am." I try to hold the tears back and loosely tie off his other wrist and combine the two together.

"It's not," his voice is razor sharp, even as a whisper.

Dropping my forehead against Leo's back, I give myself this

one last moment with him. "I don't want to, but he has information about my family."

"Your family?" Leo asks, but he's interrupted by Finn's loud growl.

Jerking my head up, I see Colter trying to pull Huntley away from him. "She'll ride up front with me."

No, no, no. I push Leo aside and intercept Colter and Huntley. "Leave her alone." I pull her restrained arm out of his hand.

He glares down at me, but his ire means nothing to me. I'm already sacrificing my everything to him, but I refuse to let him do anything to Huntley. "You don't make demands here, little whore," he seethes.

"You haven't held up your end of the deal, so yeah, I do." I push Huntley back toward Finn, and although they're both restrained, she stays near his side.

Colter chuckles, and it grates on my damn nerves. I contemplate shooting him right now, but I don't even know how to use this damn gun that he gave me. Thoughts of killing Colter and running away with Leo fill my head. But it's too late for that.

"Don't worry, I'll take you to them after this." He smiles. "Now put the Outlaw trash and their skank in the trailer!" He shouts, motioning to whoever he brought with him again.

Any time we met he was always alone, so I don't know who these men are.

I'm not sure how long we drive for. I try to zone out Colter's childish laughs and obnoxious podcast that he blasts over the radio, only focusing on the winding roads and towering trees that zip past as we barrel down the road.

The moon taunts me, taking on the role of my subconscious. The one who knows I'm making a grave mistake by going through with this.

A blinking red light in the sky catches my attention—an

airplane most likely—and I watch that as a distraction, not noticing that we've pulled down a dirt road and have stopped.

The cab of the semi-truck shakes as he clambers down the stairs. "Let's go, whore!" he shouts, holding the door open.

"I don't want to," I answer, leaning my heated forehead against the cold glass of the window.

"I wasn't asking." He slams the door closed, causing the cab to rock again, and I begrudgingly pop my door open and step down the metal steps.

We're in the middle of nowhere. Not a light or soul for miles, and I look for the blinking red light for company, but it's gone.

I walk to the back of the enclosed trailer where Colter is unlocking the doors. There are no other vehicles, so I guess he sent his little army away.

As he unlocks the door, he swings one open and climbs up onto it about as gracefully as a toddler, and of course, he doesn't help me up either. My steps echo as the heel of my boots thunk against the empty steel container, each one seeming to grow louder in my head as I try to slow my heart rate.

The members and Huntley are sitting on the floor, their hands behind their backs and tied against the trailer wall. Leo and Saint are on one side, with Jack, Finn, and Huntley on the other.

They all glare at us—at me—as we get closer. A single industrial bulb swings from the ceiling, you know, the kind with the caging around it; casting ghastly, moving shadows across the container.

Colter crouches in front of Saint, his gun dangling in his fingers between his bent knees. "Man, it's a shame those Lobos took out Nate." He shakes his head, dragging out whatever dumb shit he has planned. "I was really looking forward to gutting that prick."

Saint jerks against his restraints, but Colter only laughs. "I'll be the one gutting you," he threatens.

"No, you won't," Colter howls, the powerful and irritating sound bouncing around the trailer. "First, I'm gonna fuck that tight piece of ass with the nice, long legs before I kill her. I want her Old Man to watch as I take what's his, then I kill him for taking out my Prez. Next I'll shoot broody and hot head in the dome. I don't give a shit about them. And last, I'll let you watch as the last of everyone's blood drains from their body before I slit your throat and let your blood join theirs." Saint sneers at him but doesn't say a word. Colter looks around at everyone, their glares not bothering him one bit, it seems. "But not everyone is here tonight, so I'll have to go back into hiding for a few more months and then show up when they least expect it, taking your entire club out one by one until the Outlaws of Washington are extinct."

"Do you ever shut the fuck up?" Saint asks. "God damn, you're so fucking annoying."

Colter crams his gun into Saint's forehead, the back of his head slamming against the wall hard. "If I didn't already have a beautiful plan, I'd shoot you right now just for being disresp—"

Colter's sentence is cut short by a gunshot that rings through the air and a hole appears in the side of his neck

My eyes widen, and I rush forward as he falls to his side. His gun clatters to the floor as he reaches up to clutch at the wound. Deep crimson blood seeps through his fingers, soaking them in a matter of seconds.

"No!" I shout. Falling to my knees, I press my hands over his, putting pressure on the leaking hole in the side of his neck. "Where's my family, you piece of shit! You can't die until you tell me where they are!" I shout down at him, the silky blood making my hands slip against his. Footsteps pound into the trailer—a lot of them—but I ignore them. Colter's chest bounces as he tries to laugh at me, but only a gurgle of blood leaves his lips. "Tell me!" I yell again.

"They're dead," Leo states plainly, his foot jutting out to roughly kick Colter in the side. "Los Lobos killed them when you were a child and then took you in to work in their club."

My head snaps to him, my breaths coming out short as a man with white hair cuts him loose. "How do you know that?"

"Because I took your DNA and had Mason run it. Your DNA matched a murdered family with a missing child." He glares at me and rubs his wrists.

Slowly, I turn to face Colter again. His blood-stained teeth shine back at me as he smiles mercilessly. "You knew this whole time." I slowly reach for his discarded gun. The barrel is slick in my hand. And with all the might I have, I slam the handle into his forehead. And I keep going, despite the hot splatters of blood landing on my face and neck, until I'm being pulled away from him and on my ass by my fucking hair again.

When I reach back to grab the hands holding me, I realize that someone took the gun from me during the commotion.

Huntley releases my hair and I look around me, the Outlaws and she are standing around me glaring down at me. I glance to my side where Colter was; he's laying motionless, the blood no longer pumping out of his body. He's dead and now I'm left to bear the consequences of what we did, alone.

"You know that was your one favor, right?" the white-haired man says, his voice rumbling and dark.

Saint lifts his head from me to glare at him. "You know you owe me a hell of a lot more than just one favor—but sure, Ace—this can be *one* of them."

The stranger's boots thump as he leaves, taking the team he brought with him.

I move to stand, but Saint places the bloody gun at my forehead and shoves me down to my knees. "You brought this bottom feeding King back. Almost cost me my brothers' lives as well as my own. You made me use the panic button I swore to my wife I wouldn't need, and now she's going to be calling any —" Saint's pocket buzzes. "If I don't kill you, she will." He reaches into his pocket and pulls out his phone. "We're okay, just about to take care of the last of this and then head home.

40

LEO

I don't know when things went to shit. I'm sure if I looked back, replayed all the days we spent together, analyzed the conversations that felt like something was missing, I could figure it out, but right now I don't have the mental capacity to do that.

Not when the woman that I fell in love with—despite Jack's better judgment—is on her knees as my brothers form a circle around her.

"Stop, stop. Let's all just cool down for a second." I hold up my hands. This feels like it's spiraling faster than I can get hold of it.

"You can't make those fucking decisions. You're not president," Saint seethes, his lip lifting in a snarl. He passes his phone to Jack and pulls the slide back with his now free hand; it clicks loudly into place.

I inwardly curse Reyna out when she doesn't even flinch, just narrows her bright blue eyes at Saint in challenge.

Goddamn it. Her fucking attitude is one of the reasons I fell for her, but it's also going to put me in an early fucking grave. She's composed and volatile, like a silent poison that slowly kills you. One that I never knew was even in my system until it was too late and I was almost dead.

One day she'll probably kill me, or I'll kill her.

I can see the decision in Saint's eyes. He's going to kill her.

"She's my Old Lady!" I shout before he can pull the trigger. "I want her to be my Old Lady!" Everyone's head snaps to mine, but I hold my ground. If anyone's going to kill her, it has to be me and I... can't do that right now.

Saint scoffs, shaking his head. "Quit thinking with your dick, Leo. There'll be other pussy."

"Are you fucking crazy, Leo?" Jack asks.

"Probably." I nod.

Saint finally drops the gun from Reyna's head, but he turns his rage-filled gaze to me instead. "You do know that if you claim this girl as your Old Lady then you can never choose anyone else. If she runs or you snap and kill her ass, then it's done."

"It doesn't matter who you marry, have kids with, or grow old with, no other woman can be your Old Lady," Finn adds, his voice a little softer than Saint's, but not by much.

"I know." I know it's the only way to save her life right now.

Finn sighs, "Fuck. Alright, I hope her pussy is worth it."

Saint shakes his head. I can feel the disappointment for me radiating off of him. "I can't imagine any pussy worth betraying your club."

"I'll let Allie know you said that." I look away from him; I can't help it, that hurt.

Saint lifts the gun and points it at my temple, but I only side-eye him. He won't. He may want to right now, but he won't pull the trigger. "Talk about my Old Lady again and I'll put you and your Old Lady in matching graves."

"Although." Mason pauses, startling all of us. I don't think any of us knew Jack put him on speakerphone. "If you tell her, then I'll have Allie to myself while Sainty grovels."

Saint releases an angry breath through his nose, turning to the phone and snatching it back from Jack. "Motherfucker, I will shoot you too," he hisses into the phone's speaker.

Finn chuckles, the first ray of light brightening this horrible fucking container. "Allie would take your balls if you shot her little nerd."

Saint hangs up on Mason's loud belly laugh, and under his breath he says, "She already fucking has." He pockets his phone. "Take care of your Old Lady," he hisses at me before shoving the gun into my hand and storming out of the trailer. I know he wants to call her something else, but refrains due to respect.

I made a lifelong commitment to a girl who just tried to have us killed. People don't understand the role of an Old Lady. It's more than a relationship or a marriage. Those come and go, but an Old Lady? That shit is forever, whether we're together or not. She's just as much a part of this club as I am, and to the guys, I just let a venomous snake into our yard.

She could bite us at any point, poisoning our blood and killing us. And I can't blame anyone but myself for playing with her.

Reyna stays on her knees, staring up at me with her guarded eyes as always, and I kneel to her level, taking her chin in my hand gently. "Make no mistake, Siren, you're going to pay for this." I smash the gun into her temple and release her chin so her unconscious body can land on the floor only a foot away from a bled-out Colter.

Standing, I catch Huntley's arm before she can walk away. Finn notices and stops as well. "I couldn't let him," I trail off, shaking my head. I especially want to apologize to her, but I don't know how. Saint is right, I'm betraying my club by keeping her alive, but I love her and she did this to find her family. Maybe if I had told her what happened to them, we could have avoided this. Maybe she would have come clean, but maybe she wouldn't have.

"I know." She glances down at Reyna. "I know she didn't want anything to happen to me, but remember that she led you and your brothers into this." Her eyes switch back to me, and there are so many emotions swirling in them. "I know you love her, Leo, but you can't trust her."

"I don't," I admit.

Huntley only nods before taking Finn's arm and walking out of the trailer with him.

Turning around, I avoid Jack's eyes. He was right, and I didn't want to listen.

"You really got yourself in deep this time, Leo." He breaks the silence.

"I know," I say, not looking at him and bending to lift Reyna into my arms.

"Good thing you have me to help pull you out." He picks up the gun from the floor and walks beside me into the cool night air.

"Thank you, Jack." I finally look over at him. Sadness fills his eyes, and that hurts more than my other brothers' disappointed stares.

"Always. No matter what." He opens a helicopter door for me, and I lay her on the floor at everyone's feet.

"Can you load my bike into the back of the van and I'll take her back to Washington in this?"

"Of course," he says on a release of breath, buckling his belt in the helicopter.

41

REYNA

My head pounds in time with my heartbeat, the pain radiating behind my eyes as I reach up to massage my brow bone.

Groaning, I roll to my side, memories of my last night with Leo flooding back, but I guess the pain means I'm still alive.

I blink my eyes open slowly. Squinting at the light, I look around the cement basement wearily. I don't recognize where I am, but my eyes stop when they land on Leo, sitting on the other side of the room, staring at me.

He's sitting on a steel chair, and I set my hands down to push myself up to sit. I'm sitting on thin blankets on the floor, and they smell as if they've been kept in a closet for the past thirty years.

"I can't believe you hit me." I stretch my neck from side to side, hoping it'll relieve my stiff back, but surprise, sleeping on solid concrete with thin bedding isn't great for the body.

"I can't believe you let me ride into my death, but here we are." His jaw is set so stiffly, I worry it'll cramp.

"Yeah," I sigh, resting against the bare wall behind me. My body feels tight with tension and discomfort. I don't know how long I've been asleep or where I am. I'm still wearing the tight jeans and thin top that I was wearing on our ride; though I don't think I've been out long since my head still hurts from the blow. "I fucked up," I admit, biting the inside of my lip as I watch him.

"You fucked up because we survived or because you turned on us in the first place?" Leo leans forward, resting his elbows on his knees.

"All of it," I say slowly.

He wets his bottom lip with his tongue and leans back, slouching in the chair. "Yeah," he says under his breath.

"What are you going to do to me?" I watch him carefully. If he comes at me, should I let him kill me? I was never afraid of death until I met him. I didn't have anything that I would miss.

Sighing, he shakes his head. "I don't know, but you're staying here until I figure it out."

"In this basement?" My lip curls. I would rather die.

"No." He stands and walks to a narrow staircase. "You can move upstairs." Leo turns around and stares me down. "But if you leave this house, I will kill you on site, without a second thought."

His eyes, that used to hold such warmth and joy, are completely void of any emotion. In this moment, I would even be happy with anger, disappointment, or disdain; but he only stares at me with complete indifference. And that hurt more than anything ever could.

"So there isn't anything keeping me here except my want to live?" I push up from the floor and take a hesitant step forward.

"Pretty much." He shrugs. "I've been sitting here all night searching for the courage to press the barrel of my gun against your temple and blow your brains out. But I can't get you out of my fucking head, so if you run, you'll be making that decision for me and I'll be able to rest again." With a disgusted eye roll, he turns around and heads for the stairs. "So make your decision, Reyna."

Hesitantly, I cross the creepy basement and follow Leo up the stairs. He pushes a door open and we step into a very simple wooden cabin. It's nothing like his. This one is barebones. There isn't anything of comfort or of modern civilization here. Not a TV or blanket, only very old and tattered furniture and the most basic living items. No one lives here, and no one ever has.

"I'll bring you groceries in a while. I need to fucking sleep." Leo says as he walks for the door, not turning back to address me at all.

"You're going to leave me here alone." My head swings back and forth, looking around the cabin in panic. "Without literally anything?"

"You're lucky I let you out of the basement. I don't give a fuck about your comfort anymore." He snaps before opening the door and storming out, slamming the door behind him.

I hurry to the door, swinging it open as his bike turns on with a roar and he tears off down a long, dirt road. Trees fill every available space around the cabin, making it so the sun can barely even shine through the small cracks between them.

I can run, take my chances in the woods, run for my life while I wait for Leo to find me. Or I can walk back inside, wait for Leo to return, and be honest with him for the first time since I met him at La Lujuria.

Honesty has never come easily to me. I had to lie to my clients, to myself, and then to the club and Leo, but I have to try to fix this, and if I can't then I'll let him kill me because I can't imagine a life without him anymore.

I just don't think he'll believe me when I tell him that.

42

LEO

beautiful woman I've ever seen, the most interesting and captivating woman, and then turns her into a fucking snake?

Do I let her go and choose my club, or keep her alive and betray them? They'll never feel safe with her around; I know I don't.

But try as I might, I can't let her go.

I shove the front door open forcefully, not knocking or letting her know I'm here. She quickly stands from the couch, a book in her hand, but I ignore her and walk into the kitchen to put away the groceries.

Her soft footsteps pad across the worn wooden floor as she enters the kitchen and roots through the bags, opening cabinets and setting down boxes; the hinges creak as she opens them.

"How long was I asleep for?" she asks, pulling out her hygiene products that I brought from my cabin.

"The rest of the night. Saint gave you something to keep you asleep," I answer, setting the milk down and slamming the fridge door closed.

She clears her throat. "We need to talk."

"Yeah, we sure as fuck do." I turn around and look at her, but the minute I do, her eyes fall to the floor. "Tell me everything."

Reyna lets out a long breath and pulls out a rickety kitchen chair, so I follow her lead and sit across the small round table from her. "How I came to be at La Lujuria the day we met wasn't exactly as I told it to you," she says slowly.

"Yeah, I figured," I interrupt, glaring at her.

Licking her lips, she continues, "Hector got a call that the club was going to be attacked, and he took me with him. We got out just as they arrived. I feel really guilty about that now."

"I'm sure." I slouch in my chair, spreading my legs.

Her sharp eyes snap to mine, but she holds her tongue. "Colter came to Hector's, surprising us both, and he killed him. That much was true, but he gave me a choice. He said if I helped him, he would tell me where my family was." She picks at her nail on the table, her eyes never leaving it. "I just wanted to find my family. I never intended to fall in love with you."

Her admission hits me in the gut, and it hangs in the air. How can I trust her after what she's done?

"I should have told you what was going on, but I thought if I chose you then I would never have the chance to find them again, and then it felt like everything had gone too far and I couldn't tell you."

"So you what? Spent the last two months spying on us? Giving information to Colter?" I seethe.

She nods meekly. "I tried to find damning evidence, but I couldn't, so he wanted a time when you were separated and weakened."

"So you let your best friend and the men who mean the world to me drive right into a death trap," I state with disappointment, looking away from her. It hurts too much to look at her lying face.

"I wish I had died," her voice cracks and my eyes snap back

to her. I've never heard such emotion in her voice. "I wish Colter had killed me with Hector. I've caused too much damage to you and the club."

"I wish you had died too." I shove the chair backward and storm for the door. My throat feels like it's closing up. I can't spend another minute in this cabin with her.

43

LEO

I PUSH THROUGH THE CLUBHOUSE DOOR, WISHING I WERE anywhere but here—well, almost anywhere; the cabin with Reyna is the last place I want to be. Saint's bike isn't in the parking lot, so I kill time by starting up the coffee machine and waiting for it to brew.

As I'm pouring myself a mug, I hear the front door swing open, so I take my mug and leave the kitchen.

"It's been a week, you kill your Old Lady yet?" Saint asks, stopping in the middle of the large room.

I clear my throat. "No."

Saint purses his lips and gestures toward the chapel. "Then let's go talk about this." He turns and heads for the room, knowing I'll be following behind.

Inside, he takes his seat at the head of the table, and I close the door before taking my usual seat and sipping on the decent coffee; Reyna really opened my eyes to the good stuff.

"You didn't make me a cup?" Saint looks at my mug and back at me.

"Pretty sure I need it more right now." I settle into my seat and hold the warm mug close. It feels good to have something warm in my hands, because they've felt so cold for the last week.

Saint nods. "Yeah." I can tell he doesn't really know what to say. I mean, what's the protocol for this? "So talk to me."

With a heavy sigh, I drop my head back onto the chair. "I love her, Saint. I don't know what to do. I almost wish I had just let you kill her." I pause, not wanting to finish my thought.

"But then a part of you would hate me, and you would have started to resent the club," he says, taking the words right out of my head.

Raising my head, I nod. "Exactly."

"I don't trust her around my club, my family," he keeps his voice even, like he always does.

"I don't either, but what do I do? Set her free and just let her live her life somewhere else?" I ask, spiraling into the panic I've spent all night in. "Doesn't that seem worse than keeping her close and knowing what she's doing?"

"I don't know," Saint sighs. "But I'm not the only one who should have an opinion on this either."

"We're gonna put this to a vote?" My eyes widen.

Saint licks his lips, his pause feeling like a lifetime. "Yeah, I think we should." He clears his throat, and I see sadness pass through his eyes. "Either we vote Reyna in or we vote you out."

44

REYNA

For an entire week I stay in this cabin. Everything creeks, the worn, wooden floorboards, the metal frame bed, the paint chipped chairs that sit around the small table in the kitchen, the cabinets with the rusty hinges. I'm actually afraid I might wind up dying from lead poisoning before Leo can even decide what he wants to do with me.

Speaking of Leo, he comes by every day. He doesn't talk, only watches me read or cook or take walks outside around the house. He doesn't eat with me even though I cook enough for him and make him a plate. He doesn't walk with me even though I ask if he wants to join.

He feels like a ghost. Watching over me beyond reach, but not interacting with me. It hurts.

But today I have something I have to tell him and I don't know how he'll take it. If I were him, I wouldn't believe me.

I've been waiting for my period all week, and it hasn't come.

The tarnished gold door knob turns as Leo enters the cabin and I peer at him from the couch.

"Hey," I croak and clear my throat. My heart races in my chest. How am I going to tell him? Leo paces, staring at the floor.

This is new for him. "What's going, Leo?" I ask gently, moving to my knees on the couch.

He shakes his head, uncrossing his arms and dragging a hand down his face. "I could lose my club because of you." He stops, his eyes pinned on me. "I could lose my brothers because I chose you." He starts pacing again, this time faster. "My entire life, I've only had my mom as family, and then I found a family in the club, and because I love you and couldn't let them kill you, I could lose it all."

"I think I'm pregnant," I blurt out.

Leo stops in his tracks, his eyes blinking, but staring at the floor. Slowly, he turns his head to look at me. "You're what?"

Taking a deep breath, I repeat myself. "I think I'm pregnant. My period is a week late."

"And you think it's mine?" His eyebrows raise.

"Fuck you, Leo. I haven't slept with anybody but you since I got here. You're the only person I've fucked since my last period."

He sucks his lips between his teeth and looks to the side for a moment. "Okay, you said you think, so let's go buy a test."

"Okay, yeah," I say, pushing off the couch. "I'll just grab my sweater and we can go."

The car ride to the store and back is tense with silence, but I haven't been happier in days. To sit next to Leo, smell his spicy cologne, and he's not glaring a hole in the side of my head. But I'm also nervous. My period is unwaveringly on time; I've never been late.

I could really be pregnant. I haven't thought about if I ever even wanted kids. I don't even know if Leo wants kids.

But we don't ask those questions; there's no reason to until we know for sure.

Taking the box from Leo, I head down the hallway and to the small bathroom at the back of the house. But as I'm closing the door, Leo appears behind me, his large hand stopping the door.

"What are you doing?" I ask.

"Waiting for you to take the test." He crosses his arms over his chest and leans his shoulder against the doorframe.

I blink at him for a moment, giving my mind time to catch up with what's going on. "You are not going to watch me pee."

Leo smiles, the first one I've seen in a long time, but it lacks his usual warmth. "Oh, but I am."

He is impossible. Rolling my eyes, I turn around and try to pretend that he isn't watching me unbutton my jeans and push them down my legs.

I don't even have to wait the three minutes that the box directs. The plus sign already starts to darken as I'm washing my hands.

I pick up the test, the deep red lines staring back at me, and one hand falls to rest against my stomach. I'm pregnant.

Tears fill my eyes as a mix of emotions wash over me. I didn't think I'd be this happy and excited, but I'm also scared. What does this mean for me, for Leo, and for our baby?

I'm anxious, and nervous, and excited, and that makes my stomach roll with uneasiness. Warmth and a hard body press against my back as Leo's arms wrap around me and his chin rests on my shoulder.

The tears I tried so hard to keep at bay fall freely down my cheeks. His hand wraps around mine that's holding the test and lifts it.

"Oh shit," he whispers.

"What do we do?" I ask through the tears.

He lets go of my hand and steps away from me, his absence making the tears come faster. "We need to take you to a doctor to confirm this, but for now, you're coming home with me. I'm not letting the mother of my child stay out here by herself."

"What about us?" My shoulders shake with the sobs.

Leo looks away, biting his lip. "I don't know if there is an us, Reyna." He turns back, gathering me in his arms. "But we'll take care of this baby, and I'll take care of you." He pulls back, keeping hold of my shoulders. "Okay?" His eyes bore into mine, though I'm not sure what he's searching for.

"Yeah." I nod.

45

LEO

I'm a father.

It's not really something that I wanted yet in life, but that's not what I'm upset about. I'm upset that Reyna turned out to be a liar and a snake. I'm upset that she used me and I fell in love with her. I'm upset that now we have to bring a child into this fucked up dynamic.

My fucking head hurts.

Once we're at my cabin, I open Reyna's door for her and help her out of my Mustang. *Fuck, I need to buy a new car too.*

I follow behind her, carrying in her suitcase. My eyes fall down Reyna's back; I'm probably crazy, but the more I stare at her, the more I think her hips are already fuller.

Reyna heads down the hall to the downstairs bathroom, and I stop at the stairs, not knowing where to take her suitcase.

It feels wrong to leave it in the downstairs room, but I also don't want to share a bed with her. I might wake up with a knife in my chest.

I settle on leaving it in the downstairs room. We're not together, so it's normal for us to not share a room anymore.

I need to talk to Saint. Pulling out my phone, I deftly land on the couch and pull up Saint's contact.

My heart beats out of my chest as the phone rings in my ear.

"What's up?" Saint picks up, his throaty voice only making me more nervous. I don't know how he's going to react to my news.

"Um," I pause. With a sigh, I just come out with it. "Reyna's pregnant."

There is a long silence between us before Saint finally sighs, "Fuck."

"Yup." I feel a fresh wave of stress crash over me and I drop my head to the back of the couch and squeeze my eyes shut. The only thing I want right now is to break down, but I can't. I have to hold it together for my club and for my new baby.

"We were never going to vote you out, brother. I was talking out of anger, but we will have to discuss Reyna as a club," he says evenly.

"I understand." Footsteps sound down the hall, but I ignore her. I can't deal with her too right now.

"Has a doctor confirmed the pregnancy?" he asks.

"No. We just took the test. We'll do that on Monday." I rub between my eyebrows with my index finger, trying to rub away the pain.

"You know the guys will question the paternity. Do you have any doubts?"

The couch dips beside me. Why is she sitting next to me? "Not really," I say slowly.

"But you're not one hundred percent," Saint deducts. "You should get her tested after you confirm the pregnancy with a doctor."

"Okay, I'll talk to her about it." I hear Reyna sigh beside me and I know she's rolling her eyes.

"I wish I could say I was happy for you, brother." I haven't heard remorse in Saint's voice in a while, and I don't like when it's directed at me.

"Me too," I say before we say our goodbyes and hang up.

"We should talk." Reyna's voice grates against my nerves, but I raise my head and turn my body to look at her.

"Yeah." I lean back against the armrest of the couch.

"Betraying you is the biggest mistake I've ever made. I've never regretted anything more." She crosses her bare legs under her, her piercing blue eyes boring into mine. I don't want to let her in.

"More than getting pregnant?" I hedge and Reyna nods. "I'm going to ask you something and you have to be completely honest with me, no matter what the answer is."

"I promise," she answers. I don't know if I should trust her, but I have to know.

Sighing, I ask. "If I had told you we found your family and they were dead, would you have told me about your deal with Colter?"

"Yes," she says too quickly. I shake my head, disappointed. Of course she would lie again. "I wanted to tell you. It broke my heart to lie to you and know what I was leading you to. I almost told you so many times, like when I found out Huntley was going with us. But I've never had a family before, Leo. I've always been alone." Tears well in her eyes, and I start to believe what she's saying. "I wanted my family so badly that I was willing to sacrifice the only man I've ever loved. I deserved to die that night, but if I had, then I wouldn't have this chance to have a family now; even if it's just our baby and me."

As much as my brain yells at me not to, I believe her. And maybe that'll get me killed, but I can't abandon her now like my father did to me.

"If the club doesn't vote you in, we'll have to leave." I lean forward and rest my elbows on my knees.

Reyna springs forward and her loose hair sweeps across my arm. "They're kicking you out of the club?"

"No." I shake my head and lean back against the couch. My nerves are causing me to fidget, refusing to let my body stay still. "It would just be best if we left. The club would never accept you and there would always be a giant crack in the ground that I'd have to straddle."

"But they're your family." Her soft hand gently touches my arm and I bolt off of the couch, putting as much space between us as I can.

I pace on the other side of the coffee table from her. "The baby is the most important thing right now."

Reyna moves to sit on the edge of her seat, closing some of the gap between us as subtly as she can. "What can I do to make this right and keep us here?"

I stop in the center of the room and turn my body to face her. She looks small as she sits in front of me, her shoulders slumped forward slightly and her hair hanging in her face. She reminds me of when I thought I was saving her at La Lujuria. "You need to apologize."

46

———

REYNA

My eyes track the small trails the residual raindrops make as they slide down the passenger window of Leo's Mustang.

The speakers thud with the bass from "Pictures on My Wall" by Lithe, but it's nice. The music means that Leo and I don't have to talk, and I can agonize over what I'm going to say once we get there.

Unfortunately, even by the time we've pulled into Finn and Huntley's driveway, I still don't know how I'm going to apologize to them.

"Are you ready?" Leo's voice breaks the silence, but I can't look away from the front door.

I shake my head. "How are they supposed to forgive me when you haven't?"

"You're not here to get their forgiveness, you're here to apologize. And once you realize that forgiveness is earned and not given, then people will start forgiving you," he snaps, and I close my eyes to keep the tears at bay. I've become slightly more emotional since finding out I was pregnant, but I can't really blame how I'm feeling right now on pregnancy hormones. I just feel like shit. I betrayed the only people who

232

ever really cared about *me,* and that makes me hate myself. I didn't think I was going to be around to receive their judgment.

I'm not prepared to answer for my sins.

Leo's door opens and closes and with one last deep breath, I reach to open my door as well. As I'm placing my feet on the ground, Leo rounds the car and holds the door, closing it behind me as I step out.

Loud barking leaks out of the house as we take the steps on the wide front porch, and with a shaking hand, I knock on the large, bright white door.

Noctem's black muzzle wedges in the crack as the door slowly opens, her nose wiggling as she sniffs the air furiously. As the door opens the rest of the way, Finn appears, holding Noctem by the collar. "Back, Noctem," he orders, and she takes two steps back before sitting and watching us closely.

Slowly, I look away from Huntley's literal guard dog and face her husband. I don't know who I'm more afraid of.

Predictably, he narrows his dark blue eyes into slits as he glares at me, his thick arms hanging loosely at his sides.

We stare at each other for a long time, before he finally steps aside to let us in. I was starting to think he was going to make me apologize on the porch, but both he and Huntley agreed I could come and talk to them. I guess that's a good start, right? That they're willing to hear what I have to say?

Leo nudges my lower back when I don't move, and I finally look away from Finn and take a step into their house. My eyes betray me and drift over to the couch where Huntley and I sat and watched movies when the club went out of state the first time. The night that I was so worried about Leo and when I realized for the first time in my life I had a genuine friend.

My gut twists, and I quickly look away. Huntley walks out from the hallway as the front door closes and Noctem's soft fur grazes across my fingertips as she sniffs me and then leaves to accompany Huntley.

Their house is warm and the spicy aroma of their dinner still lingers in the air. And when Huntley just stares at me with a neutral face, I realize the silence and look around to notice that everyone is watching me.

I suppose I'm calling the shots here then. "Can I talk to you, Huntley?" I ask, crossing my arms to keep them from trembling and faking my normal confidence. The truth is, I'm nervous. I've never had to apologize, and I've never cared if I've ruined a relationship or friendship. But now I care a lot.

Huntley nods. "Sure." She looks at the guys and then back at me. "We can go out back and talk."

"Absolutely not," Finn barks, and I hear his heavy footsteps approaching behind me. I steel myself for him to grab me or hit me or something, but it doesn't come. Instead, he walks past me to Huntley.

"I'll take Noctem and we'll be in the backyard. I'm fine." She cocks her head and gives him a no shit look.

Finn turns to glare at me over his shoulder, a warning no doubt, but he relents. "Fine."

Noctem's nails tap against the wooden deck as Huntley slides the door closed. The sun is barely hanging on through the clouds, letting the smallest amount of light shine over the vast backyard.

Huntley picks up a worn tennis ball and shows it to Noctem as the wind picks up, gusting over us and causing me to shove my hands into my hoodie pocket. She launches the ball deep into the yard, the thick sleeve of what I assume is Finn's sweater falling down her thin arms, and Noctem takes off at top speed to retrieve it.

"I never meant for you to get hurt. You were the only true friend I've ever had." I keep my eyes trained forward, watching

Noctem snatch the ball off the ground and start back at a break-neck pace.

"But you meant to hurt Leo, and my Old Man, and all of their brothers? You could have lived with yourself if they had died?" I see her watch me from the corner of my eyes, and after a deep breath, I'm able to gather enough courage to face her.

"Yes, I did. I was so desperately in search of family that I didn't even realize when I had one right in front of me. I should have trusted you and Leo more. I should have let you in and asked for your help to find my family." Noctem drops the ball into Huntley's hand and she tosses it again, the rapid tapping of Noctem's nails following her down the steps. "I didn't intend to fall in love with Leo, and I certainly didn't intend to find a friend in you." I turn back toward the railing to watch Noctem. "And to answer your other question, no, I don't think I could have lived with myself. I don't think I could have carried the grief of leaving you and Allie a widow, but mostly, I don't think I could have lived knowing that Leo wasn't in this world anymore. That such a vibrant life had been snuffed out, and that I helped."

Huntley throws the ball again. "I know you tried to protect me from Colter."

"I never would let him touch you. I don't know what I would have done, but I would have found a way to keep him from hurting you," I swear, my gut boiling over again at the reminder of him touching her. What a vile man. I hate myself even more for ever getting involved with him. "I know we won't be friends again, but I wanted you to know that I'm truly, deeply sorry for betraying you."

"I know you are." Huntley tucks her hands into the sleeves as the wind picks up. "And in time, you'll be able to prove that to me and Leo and the club, but I'm still your friend, Reyna."

I face the yard, tears welling in the bottoms of my eyes. "I could really use a friend right now." I try to keep my voice from shaking.

"I know," Huntley chuckles.

"I'm pregnant," I confess. I need to tell someone. I need Huntley to tell me how badly Leo and I messed up or how happy she is for us. Something other than Leo's straight faced promise to take care of us. I don't know how to feel about it. I want to be happy, but I need someone to tell me if I'm crazy for that.

Huntley is silent and when disappointment washes over me, I realize that despite everything going on, I'm excited about our baby.

"I am too," Huntley says so softly that it almost disappears in the wind.

My head snaps to her. The tears I was keeping at bay spill down my face and I pull her into a hug.

Huntley's loud laughter fills my ears and warms my heart, and I hug her tighter.

Pulling away, I wipe my eyes. "I need to talk to your husband now," I sigh.

"That's gonna be fun," she says sarcastically, raising her brows.

"Yeah," I agree, and with a deep breath, I head for the door to go back inside.

The guys are leaning against the kitchen island, holding beer bottles. Of course, Finn was watching us like a hawk. Huntley walks in behind me, along with Noctem, who immediately goes straight to her water bowl.

Finn glares at me by the door as Huntley steps under his thick arm, but his eyes soften as he looks down at her. "Did you forgive her?" he asks softly. She nods, snuggling into his side, and he looks back at me. "Then I do too," he pauses, taking a breath before continuing. "But if you ever put her in danger again." His eyes slide to Leo, then back to me. "You'll answer to me."

I look away from Finn and lock my eyes on Leo's instead. It's more important he hears this than Finn. "I will never do anything to hurt her or the club again."

Huntley and Finn are beautiful together. Their love radiates off of them as they stand entwined with one another, whereas Leo and I are awkward: standing too far apart and exchanging loaded glances.

"Did you tell him?" Huntley grins, her pink lips shining in the kitchen light.

Finn nods. "He thinks you and Reyna might be due around the same time."

Huntley's head snaps to me and her eyes widen. "You didn't tell me that!"

"We haven't been to the doctor, so I don't know my due date. When's yours?" I cross my arms over my chest.

"August 7th." Huntley beams and for the first time ever, I see Finn smile so wide, all of his blinding, white teeth shine. They're so excited, and that brings me so much joy. I hope Leo and I can be that excited for our baby.

"Come on, Reyna, we still have one more stop on your apology tour," Leo says before he approaches Huntley with his arms wide. "I'm so happy for you both and I hope your baby doesn't look like it's ugly father." He hugs Huntley tightly before delivering the last line, which earns him a shove from Finn.

"We're gonna make some beautiful babies." He grins widely.

Huntley holds Leo's arms, staring into his eyes. "I'm happy for you and Reyna, too."

Leo nods but doesn't reply, and I follow behind him as he heads for the door, waving a meek goodbye.

The sun has set, and the last of the sun's rays are quickly leaving the sky as we walk across the wide driveway to Leo's

Mustang. He opens the door for me and closes it behind me without a word, and I can't take it anymore.

He gets in, starts the engine, and slowly rolls out of the driveway. "I can't do this anymore, Leo," I admit, staring at my hands in my lap.

"You'll have to be more specific than that, Reyna," his voice sounds bored, monotonous.

I turn completely toward him. His jaw hardens as he stares at the road ahead. "I love you, Leo, and I can't put it aside any longer. I'm sorry for betraying you and I know you don't trust me, but please believe me when I say that I will never do anything to make you second guess me again."

His eyes briefly flutter closed as he shakes his head. "You can't say that, Reyna."

"Say what?" I lean toward him. I need him to believe me. "That I love you or that I won't betray you again? I know I mean both of them."

Leo softly pulls the car over to the side of the road, and I look around hesitantly. Surely he wouldn't throw me out, right? He rubs roughly at his eyes. "You can't tell me you love me."

"But I do, Leo. Tell me you love me too. I know you do." My heart beats out of my chest. I've never let myself think about the fact that he loved me, but I always secretly felt that he did.

His hands drop and he looks at me, dumbfounded. "Of course I love you. I've loved you since the day I met you, crying and cowering on that stained mattress. I love verbally sparring with you, and when you put others in their place with only a look. I love your demeaning nicknames for me and the way you only open up with me and Huntley. I love how you try to silently protect us because you think showing any human emotion is a weakness. I love that you came into my life as a closed bud and under my touch, your petals opened and you bloomed into a beautiful flower. But then you started to wilt, and you broke my fucking heart when I found out you were a liar." He sucks his lips between his teeth and looks away. "So no, don't tell me you love me because I won't be able to take it when you lie to me again."

Desperately, I take his face in my hands and force him to look at me. "Look at me when I tell you this, really look at me." I bring our faces together, his soft hair tickling my forehead. "I love you and I will never lie to you again, no matter how much the truth hurts or how ugly it is. You saw me in the dark when no one was watching. Now I want to show you the woman I want to be. The woman you deserve at your side." The zipper of his cut scrapes against my elbow as his chest rises quickly, but I hold on to him, staring into the mess of emotions that whirl in his eyes. "Please give me one chance to show you that I can love you the way you deserve to be loved."

His eyes close and he sighs, and one hand clamps strongly around my wrist, holding onto me like a lifeline. "One chance," he whispers. "But if you put me or our baby in danger, I won't hesitate this time." His eyes open and his voice strengthens. He means it.

"I promise, but you can't put us in danger either," I counter.

"You have my word." His eyes finally soften, and I release a breath that I feel like I've been holding since we left for California together.

47

REYNA

Even though I feel emotionally wiped after talking to Huntley and Finn, I want to get the rest of my apologies over with tonight.

There's one small opening in the trees where you can see the mountain range in the distance at the side of the clubhouse compound. The sun has sunk behind them, backlighting them black and a deep orange hovers just above the mountains, bleeding into a dark navy the further up you look.

I take a deep breath, looking out over the serene landscape, trying to harness just a fraction of its calmness. The world looks so much different on the mainland than it did on Martin Island. I never want to go back. I never want to leave this.

"You can't stand out here all night," Leo says softly, taking my hand in his and pulling me toward the door.

Saint leans against the bar haughtily, his arms crossed over his chest and his head cocked to the side. "I hope you don't mind that I didn't bring my Old Lady. She's still quite pissed, and she doesn't have a long fuse when it comes to her husbands." He glares at me as we walk across the large room to him.

"I understand you don't want to be here," I start.

Saint pushes off the bar and closes the gap between us. "No, I don't fucking want to be here," he snaps. "The last time I was around you, you tried to have us all killed and damn near succeeded."

This man could flay a person with his icy glare, and I can't help but look to the floor, before I remember that I'm not that type of woman. I don't back down from any man; no matter how powerful or intimidating. Licking my lips, I hold his stare, even though it rocks me to my core. "I won't try to convince you that I thought I was doing what was right or that I won't betray you again, because you won't believe that. I was trying to get information from someone that I should have stayed away from, and I put your club in jeopardy to do so. There's no forgiving that." I squeeze my fingers in my hand to keep anyone from noticing them shaking and continue. "But things have changed. I was lying to myself the entire time I was here. I wouldn't let myself admit that I wanted to be on your side because I needed to be against you, but I'm not lying to myself anymore. I want to build a family, and I don't want Leo to have to choose between his family and ours. I will do whatever it takes to keep peace between us. I know you can't trust me, but in time, I hope you will see that I will not back down on my word to you now."

Silence hangs between us for a long time before Saint's eyes soften, and he nods. "I respect you owning up to your shit, but that's only the beginning on a long fucking road to my trust. We're going to treat you like a club prospect, only worse. Until further notice, you're not allowed in my clubhouse or anywhere else the club is gathering unless the host has given you permission. You're no longer allowed to come on club runs. As a matter of fact, no Old Ladies are coming along anymore." He looks at Leo. "You don't tell her a fucking thing about club business. Not what we've got going on, not where we're going, not a single fucking thing," he sighs. "Are you still making her your Old Lady?"

"As far as I'm concerned, she already is." Leo holds his head high, never cowering to his president.

Saint's jaw works as he chews on the inside of his cheek. "Even if this baby isn't yours?"

"Yes," he states plainly.

"I'll get a paternity test. This is Leo's baby." I'm starting to get offended by everyone questioning me, but I suppose it's slightly valid given my previous lies.

Saint looks between us and nods. "We can talk again after the test results come back. I have to get home before my wife thinks I've been ambushed again." Saint glares at me once more before walking around us and toward the door.

"Where's Jack?" Leo shouts at him, turning around.

Without looking back, Saint shrugs. "I don't know, not here." He doesn't stop, as he opens the door and heads out into the night.

Leo pulls his phone from his pocket. "He said he'd be here." I barely hear the voicemail tone a second after Leo puts the phone to his ear. "I guess we can talk to him tomorrow," he says, hitting the end button on the screen and sliding the phone away.

EPILOGUE

REYNA

"Hey, wake up, Siren. I've already let you sleep too long and we're gonna be late," Leo's soft whisper tickles my ear and I scrunch my closed eyes before opening them.

The golden, setting sun shines into the living room through the large windows, and I realize that it's already evening. "I only meant to take a quick nap." I push myself up to sit on the couch where I laid down three hours ago.

"I know," Leo chuckles. "The doctor said you'd be more tired, and you took that as a challenge."

"I am growing an entire human, after all. What are you doing?" I tease playfully. It's been three days since we confirmed that I'm pregnant, and we have scheduled the paternity test for two weeks from now, but I already know what the result will be.

"While you were lazing around, I was in the kitchen slaving over the stove." Leo's smile shines brighter than the sun that's illuminating his handsome face.

"We were in charge of the salad," I try to keep my face straight.

"And the cranberry sauce!" His hazel eyes widen, and I

finally crack, a small smile pulling at my lips. "I had to cut it into even slices."

Things have been a lot better between us, in that I mean he doesn't glare at me every time he looks at me and we can joke with each other like we used to. I know it's going to take time to get back what we had, but I think we're headed in the right direction.

Since confirming my pregnancy, Leo has been giddy with excitement. I've already caught him looking at nursery themes, though I didn't tell him I saw.

"Thank you for taking care of all that." I smile and roll my eyes.

"Someone had to. If we show up empty-handed, we'll probably never be invited back." I shove Leo's shoulder and he smirks as he uses the momentum to stand. "Hurry up. I don't want to be the last ones there." He extends his hand for me and I gratefully take it and head for my room. We're not sharing a room yet, but judging by the looks he gives me when he thinks I'm not looking, I'll be back in the loft in no time.

I'm not upset with how our relationship is right now. I know it's only temporary and that we'll be better than we used to be soon. I have to earn his trust back and he needs to see that I won't hurt him again. This isn't something that can be rushed. We don't just have ourselves to focus on anymore. We want to build a lasting relationship, not a fragile one.

Thanksgiving is at Finn and Huntley's, and although Leo won't fess up, I think they only offered to host it so that I could come. It was either their house, ours, or not have a club dinner at all, and we don't have enough room for everyone and their families.

Finn and Huntley's curved driveway is full of cars and through the large living room windows, people mingle. The house looks warm and inviting, and I can't wait for my first Thanksgiving. At the club, we didn't do anything, but the staff working would usually do a small meal for them, me, and Hector if he was working, before all the girls arrived.

I'm excited to experience Thanksgiving like in the movies.

Headlights flash in the rearview mirror as I wait for Leo to open my door, and I look back. Jack gets out of his pickup, hurrying around to the passenger side to open it for Leo's mom.

Smiling, I get out when Leo opens my door. "How's my grand baby?" Lucia coos, reaching for me.

"Hi, Ma. Missed you too." Leo holds the door open, pouting.

"Hi, Lucia." I smile and accept her hug. Leo couldn't wait to call her after the appointment and she cried over the phone, and then she brought over everything she kept from Leo's childhood.

She said she was excited to finally have a daughter and that she can't wait to have a grand baby. I couldn't look her in the eyes for the rest of the night since I almost left her without her son.

"And hello, Son." She lets go of me to hug Leo, standing on her toes to kiss his cheek.

Leo lets go of her and claps Jack's arm. "Thanks for picking her up."

"Why wouldn't I bring mom to Thanksgiving dinner?" Jack smiles at her and I almost faint. Has he ever smiled before? Lucia pats Jack's cheek, smiling a motherly smile.

"Come on, honey, let's go feed my grandson." Lucia loops my arm into hers and we walk toward the porch together.

"Ma, she's only four weeks, We don't know what it is yet," Leo hollers behind us.

Lucia pats my hand, smiling at me. "I already know. It's a boy."

I lean closer to her cheek, keeping my face forward. "I think it's a boy, too." We laugh together as we take the steps to the wide porch.

Echoing laughter and the sound of the football game on the TV welcome us in as we open the front door and step inside. Everyone is here.

Huntley stands over the oven with a giant blonde man. "Is that Huntley's dad?" I ask, leaning into Leo so he can hear me.

He loops his arm around my waist and pulls me to his side and away from his mother. "No." He shakes his head. "That's Finn's dad, Randy." Leo scans the large living and kitchen area. He points to another blonde standing in front of the TV with Finn and Callum. "That's Huntley's dad."

"I should have known. They have the same white hair." I watch Finn and his father-in-law talk, holding beers and watching the game. Jack and Lucia walk past us and toward the appetizers sitting on the kitchen island.

Leo points to a brunette boy, probably still in high school, sitting next to Mason at the kitchen table. "That's Mason's little brother, and his parents," he trails off, looking around. "Ah!" He moves his finger to an older couple standing with Allie and Saint by the kitchen island "Are there." We take a few more steps. "And it looks like Reese and her parents are sitting out on the deck." I glance over to the side and sure enough, Reese is sitting outside around a table with a blonde woman and a man with the same copper hair as her, her usually bitchy face in place.

I'll steer clear of her tonight as much as possible. If she hated me before, she sure as hell wants me dead now.

My eyes catch on a man leaning against the wall near the hallway that leads back to Finn and Huntley's room. His floppy brown hair hangs in his eyes and he has a giant moth tattoo plastered over his throat. He looks really familiar... and he's staring at me so intently that it makes me shift with uneasiness. "Who's that?" I ask, leaning further into Leo's side.

I feel his chin brush over the top of my head. "That's Miles. Do you remember him from when we picked you and Allie up from La Lujuria?"

Oh right, that must be it. But then his head slowly turns and I follow his line of sight, my eyes widening at who walks out of the dark hallway.

A woman that I knew. She still looks the same. Tiny and innocent, with long, medium brown hair and big green eyes. She stops as soon as she sees me, her eyes growing in size, if that's even possible.

Her body crashes into mine before I can even realize what's happened, and I look down at her with undisguised curiosity. I thought she was dead.

"You made it out." Briar pulls away. A piece of her hair clinging to her glossed lips.

"Yeah," I clear my throat. She was one of the escorts at La Lujuria. "So did you," I state the obvious.

"Miles saved me." She looks back at the tall man, who's only a few steps away now. Damn, they both move quick. She turns back to me, leaning in close. "We found them," she whispers, holding onto my arms with a death grip. And my heart stops.

Jack

THIS IS my second Thanksgiving with the club, but this year feels particularly lonely. It's an odd feeling, ya know? To be surrounded by family and love, and still feel like you're completely alone.

I guess that's because I am alone. Everyone's got Old Ladies now, even two have kids on the way, and here I am. No girl and no family to bring to this dinner, except for the mom that basically adopted me when I met Leo.

With all the chaos, I slip out of the side door, waving to Reese and her parents as I head for the steps to the lawn. Reese does what she probably thinks is a smile, but it's more like a straight line. It's okay, she's pissed at the world, and doesn't have anyone to take it out on. It sucks to live in other's bliss when all you want to do is wallow in your despair. I understand her. I'm about to do it right now.

I stand in the middle of the vast yard and glance behind me to make sure no one followed me. When I'm sure I'm alone and no one can hear, I take my phone out of my pocket and pull up the most recent voicemail.

"You're really not going to answer, even now?" I can hear tears in her voice and I close my eyes, dropping my head back. She breathes in shakily. "Jack, please talk to me." The recording ends and I pull my phone away, clicking on the one before and putting it to my ear. "What the fuck, Jack!? You show up after all this time and you send me out!?" she shouts at me angrily. "What the fuck are you doing back here? Who were those guys?" It ends. I click on the one before that. She sighs heavily, like she's holding the entire weight of the world on her chest. "It's been years, and I don't even know if you've been getting these voicemails. But the number still works, so I keep calling. I'm just waiting for the day that it says this number has been disconnected or someone else answers." She sounds like she's at the end of her rope. She sounds like how I feel.

Pulling the phone away, I scroll all the way to the bottom, to the first voicemail from four years ago, but before I can hit play, a phone call takes up the screen.

It matches the area code from home, but it's not her number. Hesitantly, I answer.

"Jack!" the girl on the other end says, sounding panicked.

It's not her, but it is one of her friends. "Yeah," I answer, my heart beating wildly. I can feel that something is wrong.

"Someone took Sam!" she screams into the phone.

Reyna

Five months later

THE WIDE HEEL of my sandal thunks across the wood floors of our cabin. I've showered, curled my hair, done my makeup, and gotten dressed, and Leo still hasn't come in to get ready.

"Leo!" I holler, passing the stairs and heading down the hallway. I'm so grateful that Leo hired professionals to add an addition to the cabin so we could move our bedroom downstairs. If he had taken the job on himself, we would still be upstairs by the time I gave birth, and I don't think I will be able to safely climb the stairs to the loft for too much longer. Now, our bedroom and ensuite are on the opposite side of the house as the original downstairs bedrooms. Pushing open the door to my right—my bedroom when I first moved in here—Leo is setting up fans to blow on the freshly painted wall.

Shaking my head, I cross my arms in the doorway. "We're going to be late."

Leo straightens, a smudge of forest green paint across his tan chest and his lopsided smile plastered on his face. "I'm sorry, Siren. I just wanted to finish the paint before the shower."

"Well, now you *need* to shower, so hurry the hell up!" My eyes widen with urgency.

249

"Yes, ma'am." He hurries across the room, stopping beside me to rub his hand across my rounded stomach and kiss my cheek.

"It's beautiful," I say, watching him out of the corner of my eye. We may be extremely late, but that doesn't mean I won't tell him how great of a job he's done in the nursery.

I really didn't want a theme. It's not like our baby can choose what they want anyway, but Leo and Huntley got to planning one day, and now we have coordinating nursery themes. The paint has gone up on three of the walls, and then Leo has to apply the wallpaper. He found it online and express shipped it because it was "fucking perfect" as he said. A mass of dark emerald evergreens with a white fog slowly creeping down on them. It's nice. I think it'll be relaxing. Then he has to build all the furniture I've been ordering while my feet are propped up at Second. Since I obviously can't dance anymore, but I still wanted to do *something,* I started making routines for the girls. Now I sit in a comfy chair that Leo bought me, with my feet resting on the stage and I correct hand placements and flow. It's fun, and it's rewarding to watch the girls improve.

And one of us is going to have to wash all the baby clothes I've been buying, too. Whoops.

Speaking of, I flop down onto my new recliner in the living room, popping the footrest, and pull up the bamboo pajama website. Maybe Huntley and I should have matching pajamas with the babies. Damn, I guess I better get Leo and Finn a pair, too.

I screenshot the pattern I bought and I send it to Huntley. The three dots appear, and then disappear, and then come back. She sends laughing faces. Rude.

Then another text comes in, a different pattern from the same brand.

HUNTLEY:

I bought us these last night.

Great, so we're both lame asses who are bulk buying pajamas for our two families to match.

But I wouldn't want any other life. Leo and I talked about my family, and we looked into them, they're definitely all gone. He asked me if I wanted to go by my birth name, but I don't know who that little girl is, and I like the idea that she died with her family. Besides, I have the most thoughtful best friend, and the best man alive as my partner. Or Old Man, but you'll never catch me calling him that no matter how many times Huntley says it's a compliment.

We're not married, and we never plan to be. Hell, it's hard enough for Leo to get me to wear the black property band, but the fire I see in his eyes every time he catches a glimpse of it on my finger makes it so worthwhile. We both know that we love each other, and we don't want anyone else, but we don't see a need for the government to have any say in our relationship. We do what we want and what makes sense for us, regardless of society's expectations or "norms".

We're healed, and we're happy.

Leo finally walks down the hall from our bedroom, his hair wet and hanging in strands in his eyes. A deep green tee shirt and light wash jeans, matching my same-colored, tight, satin, cowl neck dress

"Hurry up, Siren!" Leo hurries to the door, grabbing my bag off of the coat rack where I hang it. "We're gonna be late!" He spins around, a mocking smile on his face.

"I'm gonna kill you." I push down the footrest and slowly push out of the plush chair.

"If you can get up." He licks his lips before they slide into his crooked smile that I love and hate.

"In your sleep." I decide, nodding my head. Yup, that's when I'll do it. He put this baby in me, which has made my ankles swell and my stomach grow into the size of a watermelon, which presses against my lungs and my bladder. I'm peeing every five minutes and wheezing when I walk up the steps to the loft or sweep the cabin. It's not fair that only I have to suffer. It's why I've been taking it out on Leo's bank account. Or I guess *our* account since he added me to it. It could be worse though, I could be carrying twins like Huntley.

I'm not overly excited about having a baby shower, but it's a joint one with Huntley, and Allie said it would be small, so I can compromise. Especially since Lucia helped Allie plan it.

Thinking of Lucia brings tears to my eyes, and I have to swipe them away discreetly as we walk out of the cabin through the new back door, and into the new attached garage. Did I forget to mention that? Right after Thanksgiving, we went and traded in Leo's Mustang for a Porsche Cayenne Coupe and Leo got Taycan. I'm not really sure why we have two cars when only one of us has a license, but Leo said we needed two. Something about a family car and then a date night car? I don't know.

I hope Lucia brought her homemade cinnamon rolls to the baby shower. Every Sunday she's been bringing me a tray of those and one of homemade sopapillas, except for last week since Leo told her she wasn't allowed because of my glucose test. I've been thinking about those hot, fluffy, cinnamony, gooey desserts all week.

Lucia knows what happened to my family and how I grew up, and she hasn't judged me once or looked at me differently. In fact, I think it's made her kind of take me in as her daughter. I think that also dating Leo and having his baby helped with that. But she's the first to volunteer to pick me up and take me to doctor's appointments if Leo's working and planning to meet me at the office. She answers any weird or invasive question Huntley or I have about pregnancy and childbirth, since neither of us has mothers we can ask. She's started taking Huntley under her wing as well.

She's been amazing. Everyone has.

I never in a million years thought I would ever be this happy, and I can't wait to meet our baby.

Pink and blue balloon bouquets decorate the front entrance of the Viotto house, and Leo helps me out of the car, holding onto my arm as I lean on him heavily.

It's a full house, but it's filled with everyone I care about. My family.

Allie flits around, directing people to the appetizer and gift tables, while Saint stands by the bar. He lifts a drink toward us, smiling. Mason breaks away from his parents to congratulate us for the millionth time and hug me. His strange eyes have always made me jealous. They're so beautiful.

Cale sneaks up behind us in the backyard and squeezes Leo's shoulders, giving him a slight shake before he hugs me and tells me I'm glowing. It's just sweat. Reese gives us a tight smile from the corner where she sits with Jack's wife. I can't imagine Reese wants to be here, so hiding in the corner with the one person who won't ask her how she is, is smart. Reese and I had it out a few months ago when, in a hormone induced rage, I'd had enough of her glares, and I finally got to the cause of her issue with me, and it had nothing to do with me. She and Cale are struggling. A lot. They started IVF a few months ago, so they're hopeful, but I know every month that passes without a positive test pushes Reese further and further into the depths of despair. Her red hair lacks the shine that it had when I met her, and the circles under her eyes get darker every time I see her.

To be frank, I didn't want to invite her to this at all, but I didn't make the guest list. It's not because I don't like her, I actually do, but because I think it's cruel to ask her to celebrate something she mourns.

Jack walks in, hauling three enormous gift bags. His smile is small but sweet. He's been a lot less uptight and moody since he got Sam back.

Huntley's joyous cackle echoes through the backyard, and I glance to the left. Apparently Randy couldn't wait for the parents-to-be to open his gift because he stands with an open box while Huntley holds up the tiniest leather jacket I've ever seen, then Randy pulls out two tiny black beanies with the Outlaws emblem on them. Finn is beaming with his thick arm across Huntley's slender bare shoulders. Her strapless mauve dress hugs her body, accentuating her giant belly, and Nik stands on her other side, his smile so wide as he beams at his baby girl.

I can't help myself when my eyes land on the dessert table. I pass Leo my bag and book it across the lawn. Lucia smiles ear to ear, a steaming plate of cinnamon roll in her dainty hand.

"Here, my love," she laughs. "I knew you had to be having withdrawals." She holds the plastic plate out to me.

"I have been," I groan. Snatching the plate from her and taking a huge bite of her delicious cinnamon roll. "I love you, but I love you so much more when you feed me."

Her smile is the exact one her son wears. "I know, sweetie. How's my grandson? How are you?" She pats my belly gently. "We're good. Hungry." I stuff another huge bite into my mouth.

"And how's my son?" she asks, looking beyond me.

"Good, ma. Missed you so much. It's been a whole twelve hours since I last saw you." He jokes.

"Eyyy." She swats his arm, and he laughs. I don't pay attention to them. I finish my cinnamon and reach for another.

"Un uh." Leo swipes my plate from me. "Food first, then another dessert."

I glare at him, though I know he's right. My sweet tooth has been out of this world during this pregnancy. "I hate you."

"I love you, too, Siren." He smiles, bending down to kiss me.

Yeah, that's definitely what I meant. Even more than cinnamon rolls.

Jack's story will be continued in The Devil Always Wins...

ACKNOWLEDGMENTS

Heeyyyy... remember me? Long time no talk, huh? Well, strap in because I'm about to fill the six months of silence.

No really, all jokes aside, I'm so disappointed in myself that OND wasn't published in January like I had planned and promised you all, and then I took an extra four months.

So I'm sorry.

This damn book. I struggled so hard to get this story out because to be absolutely honest, I was bored as hell with it. As I'm sure you're aware, I love action packed stories, and this one just wasn't that. I tried my hand at half hiding a piece of the plot, and I really enjoyed it. I love that the villain was the main character and I hope it shocked you a little (just lie to me). But I had to take two complete strangers who were both skeptical of each other and really make them fall in love, because they needed a good foundation for when I burned the house down with them inside. There was a lot of old fashioned relationship building, I didn't want their love to be forged through difficulty, but through genuine interest and friendship. And Reyna really needed to get her shit rocked so she wasn't such a bitch in the end.

I hope that gives you a little insight as to why I was absent for so long. I was struggling with this book, and because of that, I got really insecure with my writing. I almost scrapped the entire book because I hated it... and I still don't love it, which really grates on me, because I don't feel right putting out a book that I don't 100% love. But if I don't publish it now, I never will, because I don't think this story will ever be fast paced and filled with drama like my previous ones.

With all that said, I hope you enjoyed slowing down with me and that you stick around for the end of the Outlaws. We only have two books left as my creative manager (I promoted Kiersten while writing this. Congratulations, Kiersten) and I have decided to move Eli's novella to the end of the series.

I also hope you enjoyed getting to see the Outlaws building families, and even seeing some struggling. I don't know about you, but I bawled.

Anyway, let's get to thanking some people, shall we? First, I would like to thank everyone that beta read for me, Kiki, Kiersten, Kortnee, and Kolleen. I should call them my K team, now that I think about it. I always take all of your suggestions into mind, and a lot of the time, they make it into the book because you guys are rockstars. Especially for this book. I had literal sentences that just stopped mid word and didn't continue. Not sure how that happened, but there we were, and you all just rolled with it like pros.

Seriously, you guys would not want to get the unedited versions my betas get. They're real saints.

But I want to especially thank Kortnee and Kiersten. I talked to you guys at least weekly, and you always checked in on me, never pressured me, and always said I still rocked when I felt like ass. This book is out because of you.

And because of a really sweet commenter who commented on my Insta and made me realize that my personal friends weren't the only ones waiting for this book, and I needed to get it out. Shout out to you, too.

Anyway pt. 2, I had better end this so you can go about your day, and I can get back to Doxed. I'm waist deep, about halfway done, so I'm hoping to have that out within the next couple of months. Before July is my goal since we'll be moving again around that time!

This will be the last Outlaw book written in Washington, and that makes me a little sad. When I get into Jack's book and the Christmas novella, I won't be able to walk outside for inspiration anymore.

Okay, for real this time. Thank you so much for taking a shot on a brand new indie author, and then sticking with me for five books. I appreciate you more than you know, and I hope to not take any more six month breaks. I love you.

Bethany

FOR EXTRA CONTENT

To discuss spoilers, theories, cliffhanger rants, and read deleted scenes, join our Facebook group, The DO Chapel.

You can also follow me on TikTok @queenb17, Instagram @bethanydawnauthor, and my Facebook page @BethanyDawnAuthor

ALSO BY BETHANY DAWN

The Devil's Outlaws

Only The Strong

Will Survive

This Mess

Of Bikes and Men

Outlaws Never Die

The Devil Always Wins (2024)

A Devil's Forever (Dec. 2024)

The Devil Didn't Want Me

One Night

A Night With My Best Friend

Standalones

Doxed (2024)